Under Tallulah's Waters

Keith R. Jackson

This story is dedicated to
Astrid Jackson,
a life force rarely
experienced, never forgotten.

Published by DID Media Publishing.

Published January 2025

1 2 3 4 5 6 7 8 9 0

ISBN #978-1-7357732-7-8

Printed and distributed in the US by IngramSpark

PREFACE

Having spent a good bit of my life visiting Lake Rabun on the weekends, I recently became a full-time resident. My family fell into ownership of our lakeside property in the late 1960's through a wonderful confluence of luck and magic. Any "reasonable" explanation for how we acquired it might sound like fiction. The waters of the lake enchanted me from my first dive off the edge of the boat dock. A chill goes up my arms and neck just relaying this memory to you, the reader.

Under Tallulah's Waters was born out of the imagination of this bored teenager surrounded by his parent's anything-but-conservative guests shoehorned into a too-small lakeside cabin. This book came from my attempt to "come up with a story," a challenge made by a highly creative group of aging hippies, many of them actors and artists, all of them touched by a spirit of not letting an evening pass without exploring their creative limits.

I kept the idea of this story with me because my mother asked me to put it to paper. I put it off while I attended Grady High School, college at Emory University, and the Medical College of Georgia. It laid nascent through surgical internship and residency in the Emory hospital system. It languished as marriage and raising my two sons took precedence, all the while working in north Atlanta as an Ear, Nose, and Throat physician/surgeon.

Finally, with the spirits of these hills reminding me of past creativity and life's great questions, the following story was emanicipated after its long incarceration in the pergutory of lost purpose. Any resemblance to real events in this story is purely accidental, although a few are verified to have possibly happened. Maybe. If they did, blame third hand information, the Cherokee gods, and the monsters in the lake, not me.

~ Keith Jackson

CHAPTER ONE

The elegantly groomed visitor exited heavy glass doors onto an expansive hillside deck. The well-appointed home he'd left behind was engulfed in mountain laurel blooming under a canopy of tall trees. He looked out over a narrow lake with wisps of mist hovering on its otherwise quiet surface, the Appalachian air this morning somehow cooler than the water. Taking a deep breath, he scanned the scene, appreciating the peacefulness. Birdsong didn't register as noise, merely a sign that Spring was invigorating the forest.

Wrapped in a thick cotton robe and holding a hot cup of espresso, he looked down off the front railing into the lake below. He caught sight of a large striped bass cruising the lake floor meters down through the transparent water. The big, healthy fish reminded him why he chose to travel all this way. He hoped swimming in these waters would fill him with the same freedom and power.

The guest was joined by his host, a fellow European settling into his newest real estate acquisition, wanting to share the week with a friend known to be magnetically attracted to water and beautiful places. A friend wealthy enough to cross the Atlantic on a whim. A friend who knew him as tasteful and refined, yet capable of discovering treasure in coarse, less civilized corners of the world.

The absorbent robe a solid sign of intent, the host didn't have to guess his friend's agenda. He deferred joining his guest for a swim, confessing it was still too early and the air too cool for his taste. Hours remained before the sun would rise over the mountains to the east to burn off the mist and lend its light and warmth to the decking. The host enjoyed sprawling out over the warmed boards when he climbed out of the chilly lake water. But his guest couldn't wait that long.

A locally published coffee table book titled "Rabun, America's Lake Cuomo" had been left purposely on an outdoor table. The two cosmopolitan men shared a dismissive laugh paging through the text and photos, both thinking the comparison silly and pretentious. The forested mountains reflected in picturesque, tranquil waters was beautiful, the guest admitted, but Cuomo? That would be like equating folk art to a work from Raphael.

After all, it wasn't any delusion that Lake Rabun compared favorably to the famous lake retreat of European elites in Northern Italy that caught the guest's interest. It was his friend's account of the water. Describing the feel of the Appalachian lake as "transcendent," with the lingering, chilled freshness of his skin after a swim "a religious experience," the hook was set. He cancelled plans and accepted the friend's invitation to feel it himself.

The guest grew up listening to older members of his family describing the rivers in his homeland in such a way, practicing Catholics prone to hyperbole. But those memories were from before the communists came in and somehow stole the innocence and hope away from even the waters of his beloved country. The guest devoted his life to experiencing what they felt, capturing the feeling of rivers and lakes before the poisoning. Hungary was now free from the communists. He wanted to wash away the still lingering darkness in his country and create fresh, new memories. Part of this plan included a desire to recreate the untainted rivers of the past, restoring them to health.

Most would question whether the natural world could lose vitality to an idea, but he'd felt it happen. He knew the environment of his homeland was a casualty in an archetypal struggle. With the communists out of power he wanted to help fix it. Until then, he wanted to be reborn in waters that still had the capability of transformation. There's so much we don't know that we don't know, he thought. Maybe he could find the answer in these invigorating swims and be the conduit. Somehow. Why work to accrue wealth if you don't use it to pursue your dreams?

So the man flew his jet "across the pond" to a private airstrip in a high crease between nearby mountains. He was met by his host and given a brief tour on the way down, pointing out the Tallulah River, where he was promised good fly fishing later in his visit. His host teased that this river was the source of the magical waters of his lake retreat; spring-fed, mountain-filtered, and cold enough to keep rainbow trout happy. Later that night the guest went to sleep and dreamed of immersing himself in it, baptized in the enchantment.

The guest prided himself on maintaining his fitness, a passion born in Hungarian youth water polo play decades ago. Ready to swim, he took off his plush robe, revealing a *Turbo* Water Polo league-issue swimsuit beneath. It had the official logo of the Hungarian National Team on its left side and was signed by Zsolt Varga, its famous coach. Being the team's primary sponsor had its perks. He loved competition as much as he loved his country, sports being a perfect outlet for his patriotic energies.

Diving off the dock, he began a series of laps across this narrow section of the lake. His host went back inside to make breakfast. The swimmer began by showing off his "head high crawl," the aerobically challenging variation of freestyle also known as the "water polo stroke." When he reached the opposite side, he practiced elevating his body out of the water. The physically challenging water polo "vertical jump" was how defenders rose up to challenge a shot on goal. When on attack, it created more power for a shooter's own attempt to score.

Proud that he still looked good in such a spare swimsuit at his advanced middle age, he searched the nearby docks to see if any American women were watching. He unashamedly asked himself "how could they not?" Imagining them licking their lips and gasping at his masculinity, he smiled. No females in sight, he guessed they were still inside asleep. Otherwise, they'd be clutching a warm coffee and fantasizing about being with him. Maybe they're staring through a window right now. He picked up his pace.

It turned out he was being watched, but not from passion-starved women breathlessly sneaking a peek at the quintessential Continental man of mystery.

Strands of what appeared to be a threadbare, grey-white mop wafted below the surface of the water under the host's dock. Suddenly animated, the clutch of strands drifted a few feet further out of sight, back under the decking. Not a mop, but thin, matted hair rose just out of the water revealing bloodshot eyes beneath. The predator's head jerked back, ripping meat from a half-eaten striper in its mouth.

The carnivore squinted at the swimmer through reddened eyes, teeth bared, lips curled. He didn't appreciate how the men talked, their foreign accents sneering and demeaning. He instantly hated them. The creature had grown quick to hate, knowing that his anger would initiate a cascade of bad things. And those bad things he empowered filled a hole in his nearly empty soul.

As if on cue, a large, broad wave formed well down the lake. The disturbance flowed quickly and purposefully toward the area where the man once again crossed the lake. A suggestion of a large, underwater shadow passed in front of the dock of the European's home, then headed towards the guest, now on his fifth lap. The shadow rose beneath the swimmer, a wide splotch of darkness.

Nearing the opposite shore, the man turned and began his "vertical jump" exercise, quickly pushing down with his legs, widely bent at the knees. To his surprise, his feet kicked slippery flesh. Confused, he looked down.

What he saw didn't make sense. A massive aquatic beast undulated in the water just under him, its eyes focused directly on his. The swimmer gasped in disbelief. Too shocked to scream, the guest turned toward the lake's far bank, desperately churning the water in his attempt to escape.

The "mop-man" under the dock chuckled at the scene. By the expression on the guest's face, there weren't lake monsters where he came from. Seeing the man's frantic attempt to climb up the loose leaves on the steep slate embankment prompted a blood-tinged grin. When the guest fell backwards and sideways, striking his head on a submerged rock, the creature laughed, bubbles rising from underwater, gurgling out the gills on his neck.

Unconscious from the fall, the man's otherwise fit body floated away from shore, drifting just beneath the surface, face down, drowning.

The guest was struck by a cruising pleasure boat soon after, the oblivious captain busy pointing out the host's fabulous new home to his friends. The driver hadn't thought to scan the lake for submerged bodies. One of his female passengers wondered why there was a "thump, thump" and screamed looking down at a scarlet pool expanding beneath the outboard's propellers, a severed limb near the blade.

CHAPTER TWO

Jack smiled feeling the rush of cool water over his head and shoulders as he swam. It was an addictive sensation, drawing him back to training no matter how cruddy the day. As his streamlined, powerful strokes cut through the surface of the evening's mirror-like lake, a soft, electric chill of appreciation ran through his body all the way to his toes.

It was one of the few times he smiled this swim.

He didn't like that his workout had been delayed. So much busy work at the camp. So much he was asked to do at the end of the day that didn't matter. And disagreements. Dissension. You'd think they were doing monumental, consequential things. They weren't. His head was in a bad place with the workday finally over, his last tasks so tedious, so unnecessary.

And he had yet to deal with the news from Atlanta. News Jack should have expected. News he didn't want to hear.

Diving in, Jack thought his bad day was nothing that a good swim couldn't fix. But frustrations ruminated around in his brain. They forced their way past other, potentially happier, certainly more self-affirming thoughts that accompanied his normal workout. The endorphin blast he got from exhausting his muscles and challenging the limits of his heart and lungs was his escape from the everyday. It was a healthy chemical dependence.

Yet, the more he swam, the more today's negativity dragged on him. He couldn't kick the feelings away. The pull of his hands and arms couldn't draw him past.

"♫ Trouble. Trouble, trouble, trouble, trouble. Trouble been doggin' my soul since the day I was born," Jack sang in his head, timing his strokes to the rhythm of the song's chorus. He shoehorned the blues tune's lament in front of his problems, hoping, once displaced, they'd disappear. "♫ Worry. Worry, worry, worry, worry. Worry just will not seem to leave my mind alone."

He realized the lyrics were totally inappropriate for getting him out of his funk.

But the blues brought the rhythm Jack needed, a metronome defining pace, providing focus. He always sang to himself swimming distance. It cleared his mind, rarely failing to lift his spirits out of any darkness he'd invited in. "Trouble" was doing just that, though it was taking most of the verses to quiet the noise.

"It's funny 'the blues' is pulling me out of 'the blues,'" Jack thought, talking to no one in particular. "No one in particular" didn't answer. Jack enjoyed these conversations, one-sided as they were. "No one in particular" didn't make him wrong, correct him, or preach to him. "No one in particular" just listened. The last thing he wanted was being told what he should do. Again.

But it didn't last. His funk came back even after repeating the chorus, frustrations restoring his ill humor. Inefficient in the water as a result, his legs seemed stuck in three/four time while his arms marched four/four, out of synch. It veered him offline, aiming him away from his boat dock finish line still a mile away.

Summer break should live up to its name, Jack thought to himself, ranking his regrets. It should be an actual break from the serious workaday seasons. Those other times of the year were intentionally burdened by responsibility, deadlines, and time constraints, all crowding out fun. What summer shouldn't be was his soap opera of girl trouble, distance from friends, and empty evenings. Even camp counseling was testing his patience.

How could anything he'd set up so perfectly turn out so ..., blah?

Jack knew there'd be a social downside being away from Atlanta, hours from almost everyone he knew. But every other choice for summer break came with past histories he didn't want to relive or career-related internships, an early glimpse into a reality that could be put off another year.

Deciding to be at the lake was a nod to the power his adolescent self still held over his decision-making. It was mischief, a thumb in the eye of the storm front advancing over the horizon, the adult life about to rain on his joy, rein in his spontaneity, and reign over his child-like inquisitiveness.

Since he first visited his grandparents as a kid, the lake had always been his happy place. It called to him. It was where his mind went during long training swims in the college's racing pool. It was where he wanted to be instead of caught in the stop/start life-suck of Atlanta traffic. Or sitting at the DMV, your number another decimel point larger than the one showing. Or the International Airport return flight customs line, three South American flights landing before you.

Yet, as each successive stroke hit the water, his choice of Lake Rabun for summer employment looked like a bad one. A reminder that young minds sometimes make unwise choices. To make things worse, at the end of each workday Jack came home to face his grandfather, a proverbial albatross hanging around his neck, reminding him of his daily doldrums.

Likening his plight to "the Rime of the Ancient Mariner" imagery was no accident. Literary references popping into his head came from time spent with the old man, whose mission in life, at least this summer, was teaching Jack that smart people having "deep thoughts" had been going on long before he was born. They'd written about the consequences of bad choices and the inequities of life before our first hunger pain. Before a parent told us "no." Before recognizing we weren't the smartest or the best looking. Especially before wondering how a loving God could be so unfair and make our lives so tragic.

Jack would hear his grandfather use words like "tragic" and get distracted. He'd see himself as sweet Nell, tied to a railroad track, with the Canadian Mountie Dudley Do-Right too far away, and his grandfather the villain Snidely Whiplash bearing down, head stuck out of the advancing steam engine's window, evil grin beneath curled moustache as he lectured his grandson. He could hear the Melodrama Dinner Theater participants encouraging the audience to boo.

Grandfather, Jack realized early on, was undeterred by his daydreaming. He'd spent his life becoming a well-educated man, particularly regarding "the big picture." He insulated his opinions from effective debate by obtaining as many facts and enough evidence through historical outcomes as possible. He'd worked hard to figure things out, wringing as much knowledge as he could out of the world. When he was comfortable he'd acquired satisfactory answers, it was important there was someone around that should share in his unassailable wisdom.

Knowing this aspect in his grandfather only inspired Jack to revolt. He'd yawn or close his eyes when grandfather talked, pretending his lessons were falling on deaf ears. Jack would change the subject mid-diatribe. Sometimes he played the ADHD part so well it was almost painful waiting for his grandfather's reaction. Almost. Sorry. Not sorry.

Jack didn't sign up for this when he'd made summer plans. He didn't make a pilgrimage to Rabun to train at the feet of a master, a monk deciding to dedicate his life to his faith, newly arrived at a monastery. The lake was where his young, distractable mind could spontaneously pick up a dirt bike and pedal Oakey Mountain. Or kayak the Chattooga River. Or buck dance at Mountain City, even though he was terrible at it.

With time spent doing camp counselor work and training for the upcoming swim season, other recreational options weren't happening as often as he'd hoped. Too often he was stuck at the lake house, a stationary target for his grandfather, nowhere to hide. Jack didn't come to the lake so he'd *know stuff* when the summer was over. He came to unplug his brain.

But grandfather's lessons were imprinting despite Jack's defenses. He rattled off a couple "highlights" that made it through.

-Questions posed to smart phones come from God-knows where and shouldn't be trusted.

-People who've made wrong choices and learned from them, smart people who suffered the consequences and lived to tell others what *not* to do, are usually the wisest.

There were a whole lot more, but he'd managed to remain oblivious to most topics, especially concerning sociology and politics.

Coleridge's poem had been on Jack's mind. Grandfather overheard him trying, and failing, to adequately describe the glumness of his social life to a friend, questioning why he decided to spend the summer at Rabun. The man Jack called "Pop" told him how "the Rime" reflected the consequence of an impulsive decision.

In the story, a sailor shot an albatross that the rest of his ocean-traveling mates thought of as lucky. They first saw the giant sea bird with its long wings outstretched, riding the crest of a brisk south wind. It rescued them from being stalled, motionless in an ice field, the fortunate blow powering the boat and crew out of their predicament.

The sailor's impulsive decision to shoot their avian savior came later.

Soon after that ruinous act, with the seabird dead, the craft again sat adrift. It was *"like a painted ship on a painted ocean,"* the winds again stilled. There was *"water, water, every where, Nor any drop to drink."*

Like Jack, the shooter's action left him foundering. Things didn't work out well.

"You might be starved for fun, feeling stupid because of a bad choice," Pop told him. "But at least you aren't tied up, strung with weights, and thrown overboard by a superstitious crew because you killed a bird they thought was lucky."

Any reference to bad choices that resulted in drowning was something else he shouldn't be thinking about while swimming, Jack thought. Bad Juju. His strokes picked up speed.

While Pop's insights were cultured and scholarly, Jack knew they weren't welcomed around his friends. So he tried not to think like him or act like him. Of course, it was rare for his friends to have a "deep thought." Conversations were more along the lines of "Heather's hot, huh?" or "cold beer's good, ungh?" The deepest question he heard was "Can you touch bottom way out here?"

Whenever Jack referenced an author like Shakespeare or, worse yet, somebody like the economist Milton Friedman, an uncomfortable silence ensued. His friends didn't want to use their brains yet, either. That way lies peril, they thought. And it was boring. They were still young and invincible, preferring to remain intentionally ignorant for the time being.

And that was cool with Jack. He was fine not knowing. If it was important, sure. But if it's important and he didn't know it, maybe it wasn't worth knowing. How important could it be? He had his whole life ahead of him to learn what was important. For now, he'd settle for "Carpe diem." "Hakuna Matata."

Jack focused back on his swim. Breathing every third stroke, he alternated his head turn left to right to keep his bearings. In the absence of lane markers and black lines to follow on the bottom of the racing pool, it was easy to stray. Swimming a straight line, point A to point B and back, involved a learning curve. And there was no wall to push off to gain momentum. It was best to keep his inertia going.

There were positives to training later in the day. Fewer boats were out in the evening. A swimmer drifting out into open water was in less danger. Fewer boats also meant less turbulence. Deep draft wakeboarding boats making giant waves choked him on more than one occasion. Coughing to catch his breath made Jack have stop, recover, and regroup. Restarting dramatically slowed his times.

Then there were the negatives. Swimming late there was poor light and the glare of the setting sun off the water made a swimmer hard to see. Straggling, often intoxicated, distracted boaters taking their last ride of the day were an issue. People don't expect anyone in the water, especially in the evening. He wouldn't be the first boat vs. man casualty at Lake Rabun. The place had a history.

Jack didn't want late starts to become a habit.

Once in the home stretch of his long, open water course, Jack again picked up the pace. He raced toward the boat dock finish, kicking as hard as he could. Holding his breath with his head streamlined just underwater, he imagined inching past his competition the last few meters. He clanked loudly against the boat dock's aluminum ladder, the rush of his trailing wake coursing over him as he reflexively raised up to look left and right to see if he had "won."

Checking his time, Jack paused long enough to take a few deep breaths and then lifted his arms in victory. After all, he thought, he wasn't training for second place. All this work should end with a win, no matter how stupid it might look to anybody watching. He scaled the metal rungs of the ladder and fell sprawled out over the still sun-warmed composite decking, his chest heaving from the effort.

CHAPTER
THREE

Jack stayed prone on the dock until he caught his breath. The sun started its western descent behind the far mountains. Hopping to his feet, he turned and looked across the upper Big Basin, the grand name for the first big dilation of the ribbon of water that was Lake Rabun. Unconsciously, his chest puffed out as he saw how far away the opposite shoreline appeared and knowing how long it took to swim. His times kept improving despite his troubles.

But he wasn't just proud. He was grateful. Grateful for the roots his family put in this place. Grateful his grandfather and great uncle upgraded the original cabin. And, as busy as he and his brothers made life for his parents, he was grateful they found time to bring him here growing up. Lying deep within barely explored recesses in his still incompletely formed brain, he wanted the chance to pass the love of this lake to his children.

"When men plan, God laughs," he recalled his grandfather saying about

personal agendas for the future. Defending his dreams and himself, Jack's rejoinder was his dad's expression *"Expect the best, prepare for the worst."* That's what his father did when kayaking, eagerly scouting out a new river to run. Doing so helped him strategize, with the unexpected "punches to the gut" that reality puts in front of us made less formidable. No run on the river of life is smooth. Pop would acknowledge his son's wisdom, and then amplify the message. He'd remind Jack that *"all the good stuff, all the wisdom and courage we gain to become the people we need to be next in our lives, is found in want, privation, and pain."*

From that collection of plaque-on-the-wall platitudes, you'd think their family struggled in life. Jack grinned at the thought. Sure, every family has problems. Every family faces challenges. But in the 100-yard dash of life, thanks to his forebears and how they dealt with their roadblocks, he'd started at the 70-yard line. Jacks great-great-grandfather emigrated from eastern Europe and started at zero, told that "Pollacks are too stupid to hire." He changed his last name, helped the Allies win WW I, worked hard when he returned, and raised a family. One of his sons became a PhD in biologic science after failing a military physical from consequences of German measles when he was five. His son, Jack's grandfather, studied medicine and became a surgeon. Pop was proud to brag that his kids started at the fifty in the hundred-yard dash. He worked hard, not wanting to waste the family's legacy.

Pop shook his head listening to politicians say the government should enforce equity in outcomes, having everyone start at zero and finish the same, knee-capping the achievers and rewarding slovenliness and bad decisions. "Why not have families try and work their way up like so many others did before them?" he'd ask Jack. "This happens more often, more successfully in the United States than in any civilization in history. Why screw with a good thing?"

This was where Jack pretended to yawn, closed his eyes, changed the subject, and suggest Pop take him waterskiing. Occasionally, Pop took the hint and quit talking. Most times he didn't.

A sudden, cold breeze blew against Jack's broad, wet back, startling him out of the dialogue in his head. He turned reflexively to the direction of the wind, watching a bank of fog billow out from Eden's Creek. The cold water that spilled into his family's cove joined the warmer Lake

Rabun, creating a rolling cloud advancing his way. As it spread forward, Jack saw it was thick enough to obscure the opposite shoreline.

Anxiety swept over him. Looking down, he noticed his fingers had a subtle tremor. Earlier, laying on the deck after his swim, he had the too familiar feeling that he'd gotten out of the lake just in time. Despite the incongruity of the setting and the lake's predominantly innocent inhabitants, he'd sensed a predator. And he was the prey. The menace of the fog compounded his apprehension.

Jack wondered why he had creepy, uneasy feelings. Grandfather said we're born in terror and learning is figuring out we're bigger than most of our fears. The fog, the chill breeze out of the cove, the dark water, and the approaching nightfall didn't feel like a learning experience. Just thinking about it made his hair stand on end. Whether his "goosebumps" and trembling fingers were from the cold breeze on wet skin or a "fight or flight" reaction, he couldn't tell.

"Gotta stop listening to Pop and his stories" Jack said loud enough to reach the far end of the cove. He hoped his voice projected into the void might insulate the space around him. Maybe it would break the evening's stillness and startle whatever was stalking him and make it slink away. Still standing there, he knew it had made no difference.

"Rabun's freshwater," he said, again to no one in particular, his voice softer, calming down. "There's nothing in it worth worrying about." He'd seen snapping turtles and snakes over the years, but they were more wary of him that he was of them. It was too cold and too far north for gators. This evening, though, facts weren't outflanking his feelings.

A funny memory momentarily changed Jack's mood. It was the only time he was "bitten" while swimming in the lake. A bream snipped at one of the long leg hairs on his upper thigh while he was treading water, midday. Unexpected? Yep. Did he jump? Oh, yeah. Deadly? No. He couldn't think of a thing in the lake that should threaten him, nothing that could justify his sense of being hunted.

Sensing a presence in the lake was his grandfather's thing, Jack reminded himself. He'd been annoying the family since he was a teenager, telling anyone that would listen there were malevolent beings living beneath the surface. Too often it felt like he was intentionally trying to ruin the lake's vibe. His repeated, incessant warnings were so irritating that he bordered on being a family embarrassment.

Negative thoughts of grandfather turned Jack's mind to his grandma, the yin to his yang. She was staying at their beach house for a few weeks, with scheduled visits from her girlfriends and children interspersed to keep her company. She recharged during these white wine, white noise of the surf, and white sand vacations. Alys Beach, the next neighborhood over, with its white arches, white three-story homes, and their white Range Rovers and Jeeps, was comfortably far away, a pale contrast to her colorful one-story Mediterranean overlooking the aquamarine of the Gulf.

Jack thought it might be the chance to get away from "the crazy," grandfather's obsessiveness about lake demons, that encouraged her to make separate plans for the summer. He would have. In a heartbeat. But it wasn't that. Pop wanted to stay and take care of Jack, letting her have alone time with "the girls."

Thinking about grandmother softened the negativity he had for who she married. Nothing he'd accomplished in life came close to his getting "Grams" to marry him. Jack forced himself to think of any additional things to put on the plus side of Pop's ledger:

– Maybe because of all the platitudes he'd memorized or written himself, he had common sense answers when asked for advice, flexing the wisdom muscle he'd worked so hard to build.

– You could try talking to him about anything. Whether children's poems or bird watching, dry needle felting or big band music, he made it his business to know as much as he could about anything that brought him joy. If he didn't know, he'd tell you. Given time, he might learn enough to answer next time if the topic interested him.

– And if you had a friend that annoyed you arguing about things you'd rather not, it was comical to see Pop listen and then poke holes in their thought processes, put them in their place in debate.

Of course, your friend had to be strong enough to forgive you afterwards. If they were weak, you didn't even bring them in the door. It'd be better if you'd just ask them whether they thought Heather was hot or if they liked cold beer.

Another good thing about Pop was his talent at hosting people swimming in the lake. He'd done it a long time without much drama thanks to his "rules for the water."

– Don't swim alone.

– Use a life vest when in the water.

– Let everyone know if you're going swimming or boating, not hesitating to contact whoever's upstairs in the house for even a hint of trouble.

But Pop never wore a vest for flotation, swimming unencumbered and free since his first day at the lake. He never made Jack wear one either, recognizing him as a fellow fish. Years of unassisted swimming for hours at a time landed grandfather on Emory's swim team, eventually making Nationals in backstroke and individual medley. Jack followed in his footsteps, training much earlier in life than Pop, with much more rigor and purpose. Competition was fierce these generations later.

Despite their shared aquatic attributes, Pop treated him differently this summer. He seemed strangely overprotective. One day Jack might look up at the house and catch him watching the cove with binoculars. Another, Pop's friends would be out on their docks, waving and clapping in encouragement as Jack swam by, obviously enlisted to watch for him at the far end of the training course.

Jack wondered if a change in grandfather's behavior triggered his fears. "I'll bring it up at dinner," he said to himself. "Whatever's buggin' Pop's rubbing off on me."

Grabbing a threadbare cotton robe off a hook, Jack fed his still dripping arms down the sleeves and tightened the tie around his waist. He wriggled out of his cold, wet Speedo, going full-on commando under the robe, and draped the swimsuit over a hook to dry. The steep, aerobic climb to the house wound circuitously up the hill and across Lake Rabun Road. Jack took two steps at a time up the deck stairs and then broke to his right, vaulting the uneven concrete and old, rock steps that led to the road. Crossing the street, he bounded again, two steps at a time until disappearing into the overhanging hemlock and rhododendron between the road and the cabin.

When Jack started up the stairs, the fog of the creek had finally, inevitably enveloped the dock. Soon after, a broad ripple followed by a high splash struck the lower rungs of the ladder where Jack had exited his swim. From there, concentric circles spread out over the otherwise calmed water, tapering in height until disappearing into the basin. After a while the surface of the lake transformed again into a black mirror, the fog from the creek dissipating in the waning evening's light.

CHAPTER FOUR

Jack burst through the porch doors into the kitchen of the lake house, panting from his 68-step ascent from the boat dock below, his stomach rumbling in anticipation of dinner. Almost simultaneously, kitchen cabinet doors slammed shut and shiny pots clanked against the granite countertop.

"Sorry guys," Jack said, head hung in embarrassment, catching his breath. "Don't know why that happens." Hands on hips, he waited as the last metal lid stopped circling and quieted before he resumed his progress to the table. The kitchen seemed to "startle" whenever Jack entered, one of the curious peculiarities of spending a summer with Pop at the lake.

"Quite the entrance," grandfather said, winking at his buddy Joe Cherokee, a neighbor of local Indian heritage who shared the mountainside around the cove. "Good workout?" he asked, not waiting for a reply before exclaiming "Dinner's ready!" Tonight's meal was shredded chicken enchiladas with sour cream, and the freshly cut avocados, green salad, red onions, jalapenos, cilantro, and mango were there for the garnish.

Most were courtesy of Mr. Joe, a patron of the local farm co-op.

Peaking over his glasses, Pop chided Jack. "You shouldn't make a habit of swimming this late."

"I know," Jack replied, his voice flat, expecting his grandfather's admonishment would come. "Won't happen again. Crazy day."

Jack pulled out his chair, sat at the table, and stared hard at Pop. "Your lake creature stories are getting to me," he said. "With the cove dark and fog spilling out off the cold creek, I got goosebumps looking down at the water. Not the good kind. The "something's in there that's after me" kind. I know it's silly," he went on, "but I got scared."

"*Not silly to me,*" Joe Cherokee responded, feigning a B-movie Indian dialect straight out of a 1950s Spaghetti Western. "*Dark water shields sight, hides what's beneath. Fog coming in, …, something moves, …, best way to make you white girls scream.*"

Jack laughed at the insult and the inappropriate accent, glad Mr. Joe was there. The Indian's humor and comfort in his native-American skin made Jack think less about his fears and more about the interesting company his grandfather kept.

"What'd be weird is if you weren't frightened," Pop responded in an overly serious, professorial tone. "It's not just my stories. Complex life forms evolved this way. They witness the unwary get taken by the predator, unseen under the reflective surface of the water. The cautious ones learn that having an appropriate amount of fear can keep them alive. They survived to procreate, passing their fearfulness on to us."

Mentioning procreation, Pop changed the conversation to his favorite trope. "You know, Jack, my contribution to the gene pool - through you - is important." He winked at his grandson. "Too necessary for the advancement of our species not to pass on," he said, a smile creasing the corner of his mouth.

"*Oh, like maintaining the genetic diversity of the Cherokee, Creek, and Seminole Indians, so actively encouraged by Andrew Jackson and his likeminded patriots?*" Mr. Joe said ruefully, as if the scars were still fresh, still painful from nearly two centuries ago.

"Ouch," Jack responded.

"We hope you're not putting off marriage and children," Pop said, back on topic, pretending his friend didn't interrupt. "If you delay too long, Grams and I'll be gone. We'll miss seeing you try and raise those little parasitic snot-bombs without our help. Having kids is the reason we're here on Earth."

"And old folks dying of pneumonia after sick children visit is the cycle of life," Mr. Joe interjected, still on a darkly sarcastic roll. *"Biologic weapons too cute to turn away."*

Jack and his grandfather tilted their heads toward the old Indian, brows furrowed, foreheads creased.

"What?" Mr. Joe asked, shoulders raised, palms out.

"Anyway," Pop continued, shaking his head at his Cherokee friend, "you, Jack, have got to be intentional choosing a bride. Your grandmother and I are concerned your Buckhead girlfriend's too thin in the hips to have babies."

Jack's mouth sprung open. "First off, it's creepy you and Grams judge my girlfriends by the adequacy of their birthing hips." After a pause, Jack continued; "But you can stop worrying about her. My friends in Atlanta think she's no longer waiting around for me." He looked down at the ground, shaking his head. "I haven't called to see if it's true."

Eyes closed, he let his head fall backwards, sighing. "I guess she's not convinced I'm worth it."

"Her loss," Mr. Joe said in a consoling tone. *"You're a great guy, Jack. Worth keeping."* Then he looked at Pop, eyes twinkling, now mimicking the nasal tone of an effeminate beta male. *"Especially for a Caucasian colonialist, heteronormative Christian, capitalist oppressor with toxic masculinity."*

Pop smiled, tolerating his friend's ill-timed sarcasm. Meanwhile, Jack remained stuck in a funk, pretending not to hear.

"Maybe it's better she did this now, not stringing me along," Jack went on. "Things weren't working out. Every time she got into my old truck she made a face, making sure I knew she wasn't thrilled with it." His eyes slowly reopened. "I had low cash flow, too. And she's comfortable with finer things." A long pause followed. "Could have seen this day coming."

A sharp look from Jack stopped Mr. Joe before he tried to make light of the situation again.

"Too bad, 'cause I really liked her," he made sure to say, wanting his loss acknowledged, not shooed away with a joke. "Here's hoping her next boyfriend doesn't wince picking up the bill and lives close enough to give her the attention she deserves." Jack raised his beer to toast, clanked bottles, and took a swig.

"Salute'" toasted the two old men.

"Enough with 'Darwin's Deep Thoughts' and today's episode of 'Rabun's Most Eligible Bachelor,'" Jack joked, instantly improving the mood at the table. "Let's eat!"

Dinner was good and filling, with what was left of his cold, amber beer washing it down. Jack limited his beverage count intentionally, not wanting alcohol to ruin the next day's swim, even though his liver was barely polluted.

There wasn't any pressure from the men to drink. Joe Cherokee usually abstained from "firewater," using his trademark dark humor to remind people of the not-funny damage it did to his people. Pop kept away from alcohol for two reasons. The first was respecting Joe Cherokee's abstinence. The second was that it made him fall asleep. Instantly.

Most times, the men just drank water from a spring between their two houses. Cold and fresh, Jack thought it could be bottled and sold. He occasionally volunteered to shovel out the spring's settling tanks, scattering crawfish and salamanders in the act. Flavor.

The men's other beverage of choice was homemade sassafras tea. They sweetened it with honey from a shared hive near Mr. Joe's cabin, moved to his place after Grams got oversensitive to bee stings. The family's original beekeeper, she'd cover her flowing red/blond hair under a protective hood with netting when smoking the bees and checking the frames. She enjoyed it until her arm got stung one day and blew up like a balloon.

Pop was partial to the honey, with a particular fondness for its mimosa and sourwood bouquet. After much begging and pleading, Grams compromised and let the men take over her hobby. She agreed they could move the hive nearer Mr. Joe's creekside cabin so that worried moms with small children didn't see spiraling columns of bees flying from the backyard up between the canopies of poplar, hemlock, and oaks off the side porch.

Tonight, though, Pop and Mr. Joe chose to share local craft beer with Jack, guessing he hadn't had Mexican food without alcohol since leaving for college. They laughed when he finished three enchiladas before they'd completed one apiece. They laughed harder when he asked if they'd mind if he finished the avocados and mangoes. A loud belch put an exclamation mark at the end of the meal, accompanied by more laughter.

After their late dinner, the three of them adjourned to the porch, greeted by a night overfilled with stars. The wash of light from the Milky Way reflected in the water of the upper Big Basin, highlighted against the blackness of a new moon sky. The three took their respective places; Jack sprawled out over the outdoor couch and the men in thick cushioned seats rocking gently back and forth under the spinning ceiling fans.

"You need to hear the history of your family and our time at Lake Rabun, straight from this surviving witness," Pop said to Jack, knowing he may have heard versions from others, but again not caring to wait on a reply.

"Your great grandmother, my mom, who everybody called 'Momamor', found the place. She was attending a yoga retreat at 'The Lake Rabun Inn' with a rich friend who dragged her along. The two women were taken by the beauty of the lake and surrounding mountains."

"During a break from class, they rented a canoe and paddled around. Soon after their visit, this spot came up for sale. Momamor and her friend loved the location, sitting where it does overlooking the upper Big Basin. But the house on the property scared her friend. To her it was too primitive, a rundown mess."

"Those folks couldn't keep it up," Joe Cherokee interjected." *Might have been too much for them."* He paused before adding *"We barely crossed paths. I might have scared them."* Mr. Joe bared his teeth, growled, and winked.

"Momamor's friend's family wasn't handy, but ours was," Pop said, returning to his tale. "The cabin seemed beyond repair to them, but didn't faze us. It got water from a spring in the woods between big hills, with ancient stone settling tanks covered by corrugated tin sheets held down by large rocks. It had electricity, but no phone service and certainly no television. These were problems for them, but not for us. My mom convinced her to overcome her doubts and trust that the risk would be worth it. She promised our family would help make it nice for them. Make it comfortable."

"She listened to Mom, believed what she said, and bought it. Our family was glad."

"We came up most good-weather weekends," Pop continued, "doing demolitions and fixing what needed fixing, using our labor and their money. We didn't waste dollars – it wasn't ours and we didn't want the costs to scare them away. We were successful in making the cabin livable pretty quickly. Our compensation was getting to use the property. We felt overpaid."

"As it turned out, Momamor's friends rarely had the time to come up. Their organic health food store back in Atlanta's Toco Hills kept them too busy. Their kids grew up and found other interests. The hope it would be a focus for their family went away. They decided to sell."

"Knowing how much we'd fallen in love with the place," Pop went on, "they offered us the property. After reviewing the family finances, the bank wouldn't loan us the money for the lease transfer rights from the Georgia Power Company, creators of the lake. My dad was a research scientist at Emory University without much in the way of financial resources. Mom was a secretary at the Yerkes Primate Center. Lucky for us, her friend stepped up and agreed to serve as "the bank" and loan us money."

"My parents crossed their fingers and made the property ours," Pop recounted. "I was young, but knew, even then, that we'd struck gold."

Looking over at Joe Cherokee, Jack noticed the Indian shed a tear. The sight completely threw Jack, who up 'til now hadn't paid the old guy's interactions much attention. He'd been focusing on himself, his own problems. The stoic Indian's emotion made Jack wonder the reason. It made him wonder if something was wrong.

"For most of the time my parents lived here," grandfather continued, "we had no ski boat and barely knew our neighbors. We chose to go without phone service or television. For entertainment we swam, canoed, and had a rope swing strung up inside an empty, single slip boathouse we later replaced. I used it sunup to sundown." The memory lit up his face with a smile.

"Reminded me of a skinny, blond labrador retriever," Mr. Joe said. *"swing out into the water, climb out, …, into the water, climb out. The only difference he didn't shake like a dog in between."*

Pop carried on. "In the evenings or one of the frequent rainy days we played card games; euchre, pinochle, and gin. Also dice and board games like Dominos, Farkle, Acquire, Monopoly, and Twixt. Closing his eyes, he pictured himself inside the old cabin. "My father bought cheap paintbrushes and acrylic paints and told us to go at it. We did, lining the walls with our creations on cut up posterboard."

"And we ate. Mass quantities. Unlike most other people and their weekend parties, alcohol was never a big thing. Drugs either. But that didn't mean our cabin wasn't having fun. Blueberry pancake mornings were accompanied by "The Day the Finger Pickers Took Over the World" by Chet Atkins and Emmanuel Thomas. The crazy range of the singer Ivan Rebroff and the joy of "Herb Alpert and the Tijuana Brass" might accompany lunch. Funny stories broke up the games. Telling jokes could feel like competition. Most were lame, sure. But some were classics I've told hundreds of times."

"Only hundreds?" Jack whispered to Mr. Joe. "I've heard a couple of the 'Boudreaux and Thibodeaux' jokes that many times myself."

Mr. Joe smiled. *"And the Penguin joke. Pity your grandmother."*

"Lots of willing visitors made the trip from Atlanta," Pop recounted, pretending he didn't hear the snark. "Especially in the summer, swimming months. It made sleeping arrangements in the small cabin cramped and haphazard. Beds jammed into corners. Extra mattresses leaning on walls, waiting to be thrown wherever. People making do on canvas cots, others on the outdoor metal furniture adorning the 'great room' inside. It was overly familiar. Privacy was a foreign concept."

Pop looked over at his grandson. "Times were better then, Jack. We were present for one another. It's how a community stayed healthy." Shaking his head back and forth, he lamented; "Today, with people spending so much of their lives staring at devices, …, even when physically next to each other, …, it's not good for them. It weakens society, social bonds."

Jack smiled nervously, demonstrably over-agreeable, and turned his head staring pleadingly to Mr. Joe. The Indian knew the young man's wide eyes and grimace could only mean one thing; please rescue the conversation. Both could predict what his next words would be.

Pop worked years to perfect his societal observations and political rants. The miracles of Western civilization, capitalism, personal freedom, and limited government could be next, all backed by unassailable logic and historical facts. Each topic replete with examples of the failures of all the other popular political stances so trendy wish for in our fallen society.

Jack knew this because he'd heard his grandfather go down this road all … the … time. So had Mr. Joe. After so many of Pop's lectures, he'd wanted to throw up his hands and say "No mas. We know you know things, gramps. But stop. Please. Enough."

But tonight, Pop was done talking. Wonder of wonders, Jack thought. The beer and the memories got the best of the old guy. He just rocked, confounding Jack by sitting wordlessly in his chair. Pop then closed his eyes and listened to the tree frogs answering one another from either side of the house, silence allowing him to enjoy something more than talking.

Cheap date that he was, Jack succumbed to sleep soon after. Stomach full, maybe a little buzzed, the ruminations of the day had quieted for him, too. He closed his eyes and lightly snored.

Once asleep, the background sound of Pop starting a new conversation with Joe Cherokee floated over him. He moved his head unconsciously, repositioning it on the cushion.

CHAPTER FIVE

Other voices joined in with the two men as Jack fell deeper into his dreams. They were otherworldly voices, yet somehow familiar to his sleep. If Jack had been conscious, he'd have thought he was hallucinating, because all about the porch – balancing on railings, standing on the oversized outdoor dinner table, and playing in the remaining unoccupied chairs – were *Yundwi Tsunsdi*, the supposedly mythical 'little people' of Cherokee lore.

Not only were the thought-to-be-fictitious 'little people' demonstrably real, the elders of their clan were deep in conversation with Pop and Joe Cherokee. An awake Jack would have had a lot of questions, if he could shake off his disbelief and put them into words. Foreign-to-the-ear language with strange cadence filled the porch, words the men understood. It suggested a long familiarity. The two mostly listened, each shaking their heads with concern and understanding. It was obvious from the men's facial expressions that there were problems.

To the conscious Jack, the 'little people' were the stuff of fantasy, fabled characters from Indian tales recounted by Mr. Joe. They were famous for supposedly inhabiting nearby Tallulah Gorge. He'd long thought Joe Cherokee's stories were nothing more than diversions meant to entertain and distract him, much like they did for generations of Indian children. Jack understood them as mythologic beings, fairy tales with characters fleshed out by Indians and their Shamans to explain the unexplainable. Jack knew nearly all societies, from the most primitive to advanced, dealt with the unknown in a remarkably similar manner.

But Mr. Joe never hinted that these characters might be physically tangible, with the stories passed down through the ages historically factual as well. Yet here the *Yundwi Tsunsdi* were.

Mr. Joe said that even though the Cherokee people resided in the physical world, their lives were strongly interwoven with the spiritual. The supernatural beings of Cherokee mythology that helped them focus beyond the worldly were the 'little people', minor gods with whom they were most intimate.

The *Yundwi Tsunsdi* were tasked by the Great Spirit, *Unetlanvhi*, to be soldiers upholding harmony. Man's desire to take as many of the natural resources as they could to build order and structure represented one side of the equation. On the other was nature's tendency toward chaos and entropy, with decay and destruction of man's works happening quickly if not maintained.

The 'little people' tempered man's depletion of the land, protecting the natural world. They balanced it by teaching the Cherokee how to work with less, creating sustainable order and structure despite the forces of nature working against them. This balance enriched the Indians and preserved resources.

Hearing the stories, Jack admired how Indian mythology put so much importance on balance and the place of man in the natural world.

Through the 'little people' the Cherokee recognized that skill at balancing opposing voices could help not only in their interactions with nature, but in their dealings with other men. The balancing principles could also bring peace to tribes in conflict. Listening to both sides and advocating for each could assist in resolution of arguments not only with enemies, but with fellow tribesmen, relatives, and family.

Medicine men attempted to adapt the concept of balancing order and chaos to helping distressed men's minds. Crazy sometimes being nothing more than crazy, the 'little people' also taught the shamans which mushrooms and herbs could be beneficial when listening and support wasn't helping.

In many of Mr. Joe's stories of the 'little people', their interactions with man were not pleasant. The *Yundwi Tsunsdi* instilled discipline in the Cherokee through lessons that frequently involved physical pain or psychological distress. Mr. Joe said to think of the 'little people' as your stern grandmother, loving you but quick to punish if you were bad.

Because of their close association, the pain the supernaturals inflicted didn't hurt so much as stun and sadden those who'd done something wrong. A Cherokee would be ashamed if they did something that required punishment. They didn't want to let the 'little people' down.

One example in the tales of the *Yundwi Tsunsdi* revolved around the need for their own space, forbidden to the Indians. If a Cherokee trespassed in the 'little people's' restricted area, even by mistake, they were punished. One method led to temporal disruption; a period of time inexplicably lost. In Joe's tales, if the uninvited guest managed to find their way home, it might be years later, even though they'd been away just a day or two in their minds. Displaced from their familiar, a Cherokee who'd experienced the lost years were forever damaged. Not having aged like everyone else - a frequent effect of contact with the supernaturals - resulted in depression, alienation, and dissociation.

For this and several other reasons, the Indians chose to leave the 'little people' alone, avoiding where they lived. They kept their distance from their "teachers," experience showing that crossing paths with them unexpectedly wouldn't end well. It usually meant they were in a place they shouldn't be. Or worse, that they had done something the gods felt was wrong.

The *Yundwi Tsunsdi* were physically strong and armed with an array of supernatural powers. Wise and experienced, their lives spanned countless generations of the Cherokee. They were impatient with the Indians when instructing them and short-tempered when crossed, having seen the consequences when men live their lives without regard for their teachings.

But the 'little people's' appearance and everyday behavior suggested none of this. They stood two-feet tall. Long, white hair bounced off their shoulders as they moved, barefoot with arms swinging. When clothed all in white, the *Yundwi Tsunsdi* looked pure and incapable of inflicting harm. Their faces, round and childlike, were welcoming and warm. Like the children they resembled, they loved to play. To the outsider, play seemed to be the only thing they ever did.

There was a "take home" lesson in Mr. Joe's stories. Because the 'little people' worked with the Indians to remain in kinetic balance with nature and the natural forces in the world, the Cherokee's lives had the potential for productiveness, prosperity, and harmony. The Indians benefitted in ways that people today would never recognize as originating from a relationship with supernatural beings.

After hearing Joe Cherokee's stories, Jack found himself wishing he could experience such a world, having interactions with benevolent supernatural entities personally guiding him on his journey through life. Thinking about it, he recognized some parallels with the Biblical stories in his Christian faith. The concept of a physical connection with any of God's emissaries on earth seemed utterly foreign given his limited perspective. Jack couldn't be blamed for not knowing. He'd never encountered one.

It was no wonder that many Indians had little trouble converting to belief in a Christian God and His angels. Hearing Pop discussing God and Joe Cherokee referring to the Great Spirit, *Unetlanvhi*, sometimes in the same back-and-forth, was a natural occurrence for Jack this summer. Neither man seemed worried about the proper appellation given to God or the literal nature of their faiths. It didn't matter to them when debating the vagaries of life in a world created by a Supreme Being. Jack could see why.

Jack slept through the night's well-attended meeting. Not being awake, he missed hearing the urgency that colored the conversations of the convening parties. The *Yundwi Tsunsdi* were anxiously making plans to leave, already tardy for their millennial cyclical migration. But they couldn't go, held back by a responsibility they'd been avoiding. They vaguely spoke of the need to "clean up a mess" that involved Joe Cherokee and the supernatural's desire for resolution.

Joe Cherokee spoke about the "mess," too, betraying anxiety about the process and its consequences. He acknowledged his role in the trouble and told the 'little people' he would do his part in bringing it to an end. He knew their future depended on him helping to clean it up.

Pop quietly fretted about decisions not being made, promises not followed through. Although he was heavily invested in the outcome, he wasn't included in the back-and-forth. And he knew his family would end up paying the price if the immortals and Mr. Joe left without rectifying the situation. Not being included and having no say in what to do or how to do it irritated him more than any of the other parties at the table. It was intolerable to grandfather being so helpless, so useless.

Meeting over, their plans still formless and unresolved, the porch emptied of its frustrated participants. The *Yundwi Tsunsdi* left for their rock grotto home close to Joe Cherokee's cabin further up Eden Creek. The Indian walked with them, still listening intently as his long-time allies railed on. Once they left, Pop rustled Jack out of his sleep and assisted him to his room. It wouldn't be the first time Jack went to bed clothed only in a damp bathrobe.

CHAPTER SIX

The next morning, Jack woke up, rolled over, and looked out his bedroom window. The hum of a boat engine broke the quiet of the morning. Jack jealously followed the sinusoidal course of a slalom skier out for his first run of the day on the glass-smooth, yet-to-be-disturbed lake. High walls of water sprayed from the sides of the ski as the man flew back and forth behind the low-wake Master Craft, his admiring wife at the helm.

Slalom skiing was one of Jack's passions. At least when he could get a driver for the boat. Pop was hesitant about it, notorious for docking the boat roughly. He got tired of paying for repeated repairs, both to the boat and the dock. So Jack didn't often ski.

Lake Rabun was great for slalom skiing because it was such a skinny lake through much of its length. The close shoreline kept the waves low by absorbing their energy and inhibiting their reflection. The loud "bam, bam, bam" of stacked boat wakes against the hull – bruising the tailbones of passengers while the skiers desperately held on – only happened on crowded holiday weekends. Those who loved slaloming were drawn to Rabun from early in its creation, particularly up in "the narrows." It was a big part of the lake's history and culture.

There was something mystical about the feel of a good ski ripping smooth water through a turn – one hand on the handle, shoulder nearly touching the water, full speed, seamless – the rhythmic back-and-forth so clean. Attacking each side, a sharply angled ski sent up tall, nearly transparent sprays with perfect symmetry when done well.

Jack could linger in bed this morning. He'd been conscripted to try something new at work. When the wind picked up later in the day, he was to provide an introduction for the young Athens Y campers in the operations of a "Sunflower" sailboat. While it was less of a thrill than waterskiing, at least in this mountain lake, it was still fun.

Jack learned sailing from his father and the Boys Camp supervisors found out about his skill. A donor had given a couple of these lightweight, plastic encased, Styrofoam "fun boats" to the "Y." Impossible to sink and easy to flip, their small, retractable wooden daggerboard was the only thing that kept them from skirting across the surface of the lake like a pressed paper coffee cup in a good blow.

Jack remembered laughing when told of the plan. They couldn't be serious, he thought to himself. This would be a one-time deal, for sure. No one sailed on Lake Rabun. For good reason.

Jack inherited the watersport gene. His father was the first in the family to grow up with a ski boat, Pop buying a used MasterCraft 190 when the child got old enough to pull. Later, Grandfather purchased a refurbished 16-foot Hobie Cat. They'd built a house on the beach in the panhandle of Florida, the catamaran a lifelong dream for grandfather at the time. It was a skill his son picked up quickly. Then the boy was gifted brand-new kite surfing gear after showing promise while taking lessons when the family vacationed in Maui. All this and whitewater kayaking, too, with two summers spent as a raft guide on the New River in West Virginia.

Feeling the sail fill in the wind, pulling and releasing the "sheet" with one hand to garner its power, using the tiller with the other hand to provide just the right counter to tack into the wind, was something Jack thought everyone should experience. Maximizing your speed by balancing your weight to fill the sail and have the least amount of boat in the water, all with the only sound a gentle ripple against the hull.... Jack thought everything about it was uniquely beautiful. You felt a part of the wind. You had control of its quiet power, no noisy engines, fuel smell, or smoke. He would agree to sail a garbage can if given the opportunity. Just like his dad. Just like his Pop. It was a thing.

But the same factors that made Lake Rabun optimal for slalom skiing made it terrible for sailing. For good sailing conditions, the skinny lake's open water basins needed to line up with the prevailing winds. Even if in line, it was common for the winds on Rabun to be gusty and inconsistent because of the surrounding mountains. Prospects were better than normal today, though, with the winds predicted to be mild and steady throughout the early afternoon, coming in from the south and west.

Jack's other concern taking the novices out to sail was wakeboarders. Besides the occasional obnoxious teen thinking it funny to buzz by and spray the sailors, the massive wakes from those ballast-heavy boats could easily swamp his kids. Wakeboarding was a blast, but, like the Jet Skis zipping around, gave the lake a less peaceful energy. It reminded

Jack of a trip cross-country snow skiing when the perfect quiet of the evergreen forest was disturbed by the blasting sound of snowmobiles. Those machines were fun, too. But they had a wholly different, less in-tune-with-nature vibe. Obnoxiously noisy. Less harmonious. Like the 'little people' might say, "out of balance." Purveyors of chaos.

Once out of bed, he dressed, washed his hair in the sink, and put on his camp counselor's clothes. Since he was already up, Jack guessed he could find something useful to do if he got to work early. Going downstairs for breakfast, he imagined volunteering himself for "tick patrol," searching the hairlines of the campers for the blood-bloated, parasitic arachnids. Maybe he could make it more fun by imitating chimpanzee noises while he picked through the children's hair, pretending to eat what he found.

Once again, seemingly for no reason at all, Jack's appearance in the kitchen was heralded by a cacophony of closing cabinets and clanging pots. Jack shook his head in wonder, still not understanding why.

Pop and Mr. Joe had finished breakfast. It was Jack's turn to do the dishes. Remnants of boiled eggs and deer sausage littered their plates. The sun as it crested the eastern mountains shone through a window with southern exposure onto their drained juice glasses, lighting all the colors of the spectrum on the polished surface of the wormy maple table.

Neither of the men seemed to notice the noises accompanying Jack's entry, or even turned to see if he'd joined them. They were knee-deep in conversation, so focused that Jack's immediate impression was that "something's rotten in the State of Denmark." He was intrigued by Mr. Joe's tone of voice this morning, an almost whispered impatience when discussing the fix they were in.

Watching the two, Jack's thought about how much he appreciated Joe Cherokee. He'd been a great neighbor and constant friend to his grandfather, especially with "Grams" on vacation. His presence had been an unexpected highlight to Jack's summer. Not only was he an encyclopedic source of knowledge regarding the history of the region, the people, and the flora and fauna in the forest, he also made Jack less worried about his long swims on open water. He'd suggested an efficient, safer route near the bank, knew the exact distance traveled so he could compare his times, and which docks along the way had friendly inhabitants. The Indian also kept up with his training schedule, giving Jack the feeling he had a personal, long-range lifeguard.

Through Mr. Joe, Jack was exposed to Cherokee mythology, finding the mysticism intriguing. As with many old-world mythologies, Mr. Joe's tales of Cherokee Indian beliefs described supernatural characters that had special powers or unique roles in relation to man. But, unlike the formative stories he'd learned regarding the Egyptian, Greek, Roman, or Norse Gods, Jack found a comparative dearth of information on the Cherokee mythology's "lead characters." He'd always enjoyed searching what texts he had available for all the "messy details" of different gods challenging their brothers, bored gods breeding with mortals, or condemned men like Prometheus, tied to a rock with birds eating their liver for stealing the god's fire.

Not a lot about the indian gods seemed "hashed out" to him, other than what they represented to the Cherokee in the pantheon of the supernatural. Yet, even with that most likely naïve observation, Jack felt that any society advanced enough to formulate a storyline for creation and a path for harmonious coexistence was worth taking seriously. So he read and reread Cherokee fables, looking for archetypes and symbolism. He appreciated Mr. Joe answering questions and knowing more about the meaning of the myths than he could pick up researching online.

Primitive survival was another interest of Jack's. The woods were right outside his window and he had an abundance of free time. He learned Joe Cherokee had primitive life skills geared to the Southern Appalachians, absorbing much of it from his native Indian culture and honed by years of forced practice. Jack formulated a plan to take what Mr. Joe could teach him and supplement it with survival "hacks" he picked up from internet searches.

He'd seen contestants on reality television shows nearly starve when they were plunked down alone in a wilderness setting, often bailing out in less than a couple weeks. Jack was embarrassed for them, knowing how hard they trained for the chance to be in the competition. Jack promised himself that if he was in their position, he'd at least learn enough not to starve. He'd learn enough to at least get by. After all, millennia of humankind preceded him not having 24-hour grocery stores, ice boxes for food preservation, and on-demand, reliable fire to cook.

Living with and learning from Joe Cherokee these few weeks, Jack knew one thing for sure. There was no question this Indian did just fine in the woods by himself. The man thrived in the forest. He didn't merely remain alive. Jack grasped the Indian's methods related to priorities in survival. At least he understood the theory. But the reality of actually doing what the man said to do was a different thing entirely.

On television, what made most of the experienced survivalists bail out of competition was predictable, namely a miserable, lonely, bug-bitten, gastrointestinally disrupted, fever-dream disoriented, starving surrender to the elements. After being taught by Joe Cherokee for a month, with an emphasis on learning which berries to gather, what roots to forage, and whether a plant was edible, he was overwhelmed. Add to that his instructions on how to set snares and traps for small game, the best elementary gear for fishing, catching crawdads, and the proper technique in killing snakes for food, and Jack had to admit the truth. Lasting a couple of weeks in the woods by himself would be a stretch.

He'd need to skip primitive survival and use mosquito repellant. And he'd bring fishing nets and modern gear, a top-of-the-line animal trap, a shotgun, and a rifle with enough ammunition to hunt for food and protect himself. Even then, he'd need to be near the source of an untainted freshwater spring. He'd also do well to stumble across pre-existing shelter and do his best to upgrade, with a fortified, lockable "meat house" within safe walking distance from where he slept. And it would be good if he could bring an air horn to scare away bears, a mosquito net because bug spray wasn't perfect, and a reliable Firestarter.

Overall, he'd be more confident and less lonely if he brought along his new Indian friend. That might actually make it fun.

"Why not get your swim out of the way before work?" Pop asked, finally acknowledging Jack while glancing over at Mr. Joe. "Day swims are safer. 'Moonshine Bob' and 'Herman, the Lake Monster' like it when you swim late. They've been eyeing you since you first jumped into Rabun as a kid." He'd conveniently put aside his grandson's unspoken request to stop mentioning underwater demons, reflexively defaulting to warning Jack about things he was spooked about just yesterday.

Jack wondered whether his grandfather was oblivious to his feelings or just plain cruel. These two boogiemen had been conjured up by Pop when the old man was a young teenager. Alerting everyone to the possibility of lake monsters was a constant around the kitchen table for as long as the family had been at the lake. Initially, everybody figured the teenage Pop would grow out of it, hopefully move on from the unsettling phase he was going through. Or maybe they'd hoped he'd run out of energy pleading his case when no one was listening. Ultimately, they chalked up his dark preoccupations to having no television, telephone, or radio to keep his hyperactive brain distracted.

So, he kept on. Over time, Pop's incessant 'Moonshine Bob' and 'Herman" warnings were demoted to the status of background noise. Eventually the whole family learned to tune them out, tolerating the uncomfortably menacing characters of Pop's imagination as a trade-off for the otherwise positive energy he provided. Everyone knew he wanted to honor his parents and do his best to carry on Momamor's legacy of making a visit to the Rabun cabin and lake entertaining, memorable, and safe.

Speaking of trade-offs, given a choice, most in the family would rather Jack figure out a way to no longer hear Pop's overused collection of jokes and groan-worthy "shaggy dog" stories. Hearing them over and over was far more irritating than alerts about imaginary lake monsters. New visitors would trigger an avalanche of old jokes, beginning with those tried and true to at least cause a smile. "It is the way," experienced guests would say, nodding their heads up and down like Mandalorians, mouthing the punch lines to each other. Insert eye roll.

Jack often wondered how grandmother endured Pop's ceaseless comedic impulses. His father guessed she had an "off button" installed in her brain early on in their marriage. How else to explain how she'd managed to remain with him, flawed as he was? When asked about it, "Gram" reminded us that nobody's perfect. We all have to put up with something. "And who says he's not putting up with me?" she'd say playfully, winking at us, giggling at the thought.

That said, Jack was over putting up with it. He'd lost patience with his grandfather's non-stop preoccupation with made-up monsters.

"Pop," Jack began, girding up for the challenge. "'Moonshine Bob'? Couldn't you come up with a better name?" Almost as simple and childish as Joe Cherokee, Jack thought. "And your boogieman's backstory strains credibility. We're supposed to believe that a drowned moonshiner magically lives underwater like some redneck lake troll? Really?"

"I think there's a couple ways you could step up both the menace and believability of your antagonist," Jack said to Pop, mocking his imaginary creation as he went through his prepared list of deficiencies. "First off, you need a sinister name. I'd suggest 'Lake Man Dead', 'the Un-Drowned', or 'the Rabun Lake Zombie'. Any of those would be an improvement. And 'Bob' needs an origin story that works. Why doesn't he need air to breathe? What's his motivation to kill? If he's just angry at the world, what makes him that way? He's just too one-dimensional."

Jack had planned to confront his grandfather about his cautionary warnings for a while. He'd thought about it often while he was swimming. Long swims with his head immersed in water, the unchanging cadence of his strokes left time for contemplation. He'd been thinking how to make summer break more fun moving forward. The first opportunity that came to mind was Pop's antagonists, 'Moonshine Bob', and 'Herman', the monsters casting a pall over Jack's swims.

He'd be a family hero if he could make his grandfather stop.

Mocking Pop's monsters was only Jack's opening salvo. He wanted Pop to admit the monsters were imaginary. After all, Pop harped on the need for honesty, seeing himself a "Warrior for Truth." Jack thought Pop should extend his battle against dishonesty to his personal life. Pop taught Jack how hearing anything outside of an honest answer felt instinctively wrong because lies had an ugliness about them.

He'd use grandfather's own words against him.

When the old man discussed politics, he channeled "Conan, the Barbarian," claiming to defeat the opposition's dishonesty so badly and so completely "that we can hear the lamentations of their women." "So why be dishonest yourself?" Jack wanted to ask. He guessed Pop wouldn't like the lines of the battle turning on him or his "imaginaries."

Jack already had the feeling that honest people recognize the truth. Truth usually makes sense. There's generally a reasonableness to it. Pop guided him to recognizing that without truth there cannot be beauty. That's why the ugly strangeness of 'Bob' and 'Herman' seemed so out of Pop's character. It's an energy-wasting sinkhole of falseness, Jack thought, so strange in a man so wed to knowing, to whom wisdom was a hard-won commodity.

A creative guy, Pop might be able to redirect the energies he'd wasted on such negative thoughts. Maybe the ugliness of his "untruths" was holding him back from his true potential. Focusing that creativity somewhere else might turn out to be amazing. The truth could set him free.

But for now, Jack hadn't finished mocking Pop's imaginary enemies. "The same with 'Herman the Lake Monster'," Jack continued. "We're supposed to believe there's a giant, catfishy thing, like H. P. Lovecraft's fictional 'Shoggoth', that lurks in the dark green depths of Lake Rabun. It awakens, aroused to do the evil bidding of any villain who takes time to bond with it? It sounds like a dark web knock-off of "Hillbilly Handfishing," scary-sized catfish "noodling" gone very, very wrong. It's almost comical."

Not through venting, he turned his attention to Joe Cherokee. "No disrespect, Mr. Joe, but just sitting there, nodding your head, letting Pop rail on with these warnings about lake monsters, …, it encourages him. You've got to be as tired of this as the rest of us."

Pop and Joe looked at each other conspiratorially, which set Jack off even more.

"Instead of ignoring Pop like the rest of us, it's like you urge him on," Jack continued. "And don't think I haven't noticed things. It's been getting urgent and undisguised with you two. I overhear you talk of your 'little people' like they're real. It's all very weird. Why are you OK with Pop's "crazy"?"

Given grandfather's proclivities, Jack thought the strangest answer might be the most likely. Any time now, he guessed, spaceships would land on the lake house's ridged metal roof and he'd get to meet Pop's alien overlords. Or Mr. Joe would morph into a man-sized, talking tree frog flicking his tongue out to catch an unsuspecting dragonfly while enlightening us that humans aren't really in control. Maybe the trees behind the house would animate and begin walking down the hill like Tolkien's Ents from "the Lord of the Rings." Or Pop would pull a magical sword of power from the not-really-fake boulder covering the well, brandishing it above him in a golden glow of light surrounding his kingly head.

He was reminded why he was uncomfortable bringing friends over.

"Why can't he be more like my friend's grandfathers?" Jake asked himself, wistfully. "Smiling in the background – because they couldn't hear what people were saying, telling anyone that would listen how great sports stars were back in the good old days – because they couldn't remember yesterday, and serving as an occasional source of easy cash – because they were easy marks."

"Jack, you're right. You deserve to have your questions answered," Pop unexpectedly replied, pulling Jack out of daydreams. "It's time you were brought into the loop," he continued, interrupting the uncomfortably long pause that followed his grandson's plea.

Jack turned to look at Pop, thinking he would hear more obfuscation. Instead, his grandfather answered earnestly, both eyes fixed on Jack's.

"Your embarrassing grandfather and our Cherokee neighbor are indeed feeling a sense of urgency. First off, please understand that all either one of us wants is to keep the lake safe for the family. The things I'm about to tell you will sound … uh …" he cleared his throat a few times, "how should I put this, …, they will sound, …, made up." Pop looked over at Joe Cherokee, wrinkling his forehead, grimacing. "Well, …, they're not. Turns out Mr. Joe's stories about the *Yundwi Tsunsdi* are, …, more real than we have let on."

Jack tilted his head reflexively, wondering what truths included Cherokee Indian fables of river dwelling leprechaun impersonators.

"Our lake, and specifically our cove, is a battleground. It's where Joe Cherokee, the 'little people' you hear us talk about, and a dark mistake from the past struggle daily." Pop paused to register Jack's reaction.

Seeing that he had none, Pop looked deeper. His grandson's expression stayed flat. It was evident that Jack didn't believe he was getting a straight answer. "You, Jack, are going to have to open your mind to the supernatural."

With grandfather's words barely out of his mouth, smiling, round-faced *Yundwi Tsunsdi* appeared to Jack. They had been frozen in place, having abandoned their play on the kitchen counter when he came in earlier. They'd stopped rummaging through shelves and cabinets looking for polished objects, most bemused by seeing their reflections in the stainless-steel cookware.

Jack blinked a few times, shook his head as if to clear it, and still saw them. He tried looking away, but even the reflections in the picture windows affirmed the reality of the apparitions. Standing about two feet tall, he noticed their light-colored hair almost dragged the floor as they moved. Despite their child-like faces, he recognized a gravity to them. Jack couldn't help but stare. The 'little people' were real. So much for "the truth shall set you free," Jack thought. The truth just upended his world.

CHAPTER SEVEN

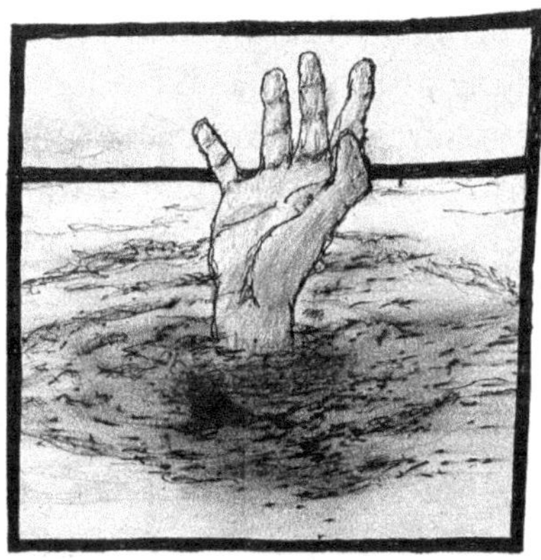

Pop kept talking, taking advantage of his grandson's stunned silence. But Jack wasn't listening. He was rubbing his disbelieving eyes. Meanwhile, the 'little people' all around him were animated and happy.

It had been an exhausting summer for the *Yundwi Tsunsdi*, trying to remain unseen by the ever-present Jack. No longer having to hide was a welcomed relief. The tribe had already agreed among themselves to embrace the youth as another, like Pop, they could trust and mentor. Now that introductions were made, they looked forward to finally working with the boy. After all, time was wasting. Another ally could only help matters.

Light-headed, Jack sat down. He tried forcing a smile to the strange visitors scattered about the kitchen, spilling out into the great room, and onto the front porch. "Mr. Joe's herbs might do this, or maybe the psilocybin from his mushrooms," Jack said to himself, a half-hearted effort at denial.

Jack had trouble believing the truth of it despite the evidence all around him. But any reasonable explanation, any twist in perception he could have blamed on mind-altering drugs, was feeble on its face. He knew in his heart what he was witnessing. There were supernaturals surrounding him, welcoming him into their confidence. It might be unexplainable, but it was real.

At least Jack knew what made the kitchen "startle" when he came down the stairs. Going through Pop's cabinets was obviously a source of fascination for the 'little people." He grinned seeing two of them holding reflective lids, giggling at how their faces looked against the curved surface. Another was sticking his tongue out at a shiny glass pitcher, his lower face distorted round below the spout. Even as active as the 'little people' were, their movements were surprisingly quiet. It made Jack wonder why, at an earlier time, a metal lid circled so noisily and so long before stopping.

"Now that you're "up to speed," there's something else," grandfather said, even though he knew Jack was obviously, absolutely not "up to speed." "You should learn the truth about Joe Cherokee. His history is the key to unlocking your understanding of our cove and its current … complications."

Pop preached on. "What we believe to be real isn't the whole story of the world in which we live, Jack. Given what you're witnessing, I presume you've figured that out." Silence from Jack. "Most people are comfortable, even righteous, thinking that everything is knowable, reasonable, or factually explainable. That was me when I was younger. The explosion of information in the sciences makes even the wildest things in the universe seem within our ability to explain. Mankind's hubris, pride in thinking we can logically interpret everything in the world around us, …, well… it's just confirmation of our flawed nature. When I met the 'little people' it humbled me, revealed my ignorance."

"Being with Joe and his supernatural friends taught me the unknowability of the world. Wrapping our heads around things that exist beyond our understanding forces us to keep an open mind. Facts keep us comfortable, but there is much more out there to appreciate, more wonders that exist than facts can explain. Layers upon layers of truths we don't know enough to question. Things that we don't know that we don't know. It takes courage to face that fact. I struggle with that kind of uncertainty."

Jack couldn't speak. His confusion and silence spoke to his state of mind.

"Choosing how and when to present this world to you, Jack, hasn't been easy," said his grandfather. "But you're older and responsible enough to deserve answers." Pop closed his eyes remembering. "My first encounter with the supernatural, my baptism to the unexplainable, was a nightmare compared to yours. What I experienced all those years ago still haunts me."

"A few months after we took over ownership of the property, I was swimming alone," Grandfather began, recounting that fateful day. "I was covered in mud after cleaning out our spring-fed cistern, the primitive system that collected water for the cabin before we sank a well decades later. The sun was high and bright, shining through the surface of the water. I could follow its shimmering, sunburst rays until they attenuated in the dark, green depths. I'd been swimming a while when I felt a disturbance beneath me. Opening my eyes underwater, I tried to see what it was, anything that might explain the movement I sensed."

"My eyes burned a little, I couldn't focus, but what looked like a bunch of grey/white strands from a stringy, old mop were waving back-and-forth in the deep water." Pop tightened his face. "Confused, then frightened, I watched as a gnarled hand rose from the darkness and grasped my ankle. I pulled away but it yanked me under the water. I struggled, only managing to pull it a little closer to the light. Its other hand reached up, prune-skinned fingers locking together."

"I twisted and kicked," grandfather continued, "but couldn't escape. I thought I was a strong swimmer, but I was physically overwhelmed. It was hard to believe how easily it pulled me down. The creature may not have been as strong, but it wasn't struggling to breathe. With one last violent pull, I sank and started inhaling water."

Grandfather's posture changed, shoulders back, head raised, remembering how he'd survived the attack. "Incredibly, because I was a goner, for sure, a flash of multicolored lights sparkled in the water all around me. Everything began to spin, creating a whirlpool of bubbles. The rainbow swirl engulfed my body, sweeping me up to the surface as the creature's grip on my ankle tore loose. Once I broke free, I choked and vomited, my lungs filled with lake water. Then I swam as fast as I could to the shoreline, coughing and scared as hell." Pop exhaled in the recollection. "I couldn't get out of the water fast enough."

Pop motioned over to Joe Cherokee. "Joe was standing on the bank that I was trying to climb. I was frantic, clumsy. Pulling on rhododendron branches and slipping on the wet clay and dry leaves, I wasn't making any headway. He introduced himself by lowering a hand to pull me up, out of danger."

"After I slowed coughing and caught my breath, we started walking around the lake road to the horseshoe bridge over Eden creek, up the hill, around the corner, and up the rock steps to my house. We didn't say a word to each other the whole way." Pop reflected, recounting the memory. "Almost at the door, just as he turned around to leave, I asked if he saw what happened. Shaking his head up and down, he said he was astonished I survived."

Joe Cherokee took over telling the story. *"The next day I told your grandfather the truth. Some of it, anyway. I let him have the night to calm down and analyze what happened. I wanted him to figure out - on his own - that being pulled underwater by human hands and magically escaping its grasp in a swirl of colored lights wasn't explainable. It couldn't be reasoned out. He'd encountered the supernatural firsthand with no preparation."*

"I knew that without familiarity with the supernatural, like the Cherokee people had in their material interactions with their gods, yesterday had to feel unreal. When your grandfather and I were able to talk about it, I held back on nearly everything. I simply answered his questions, not hinting he didn't know which questions to ask," Mr. Joe explained. *"I listened to him work his way through what happened without correcting his version of events. Filling him in on all the true particulars could be held back for later. Telling him the secrets of the cove, dropping it on him all at once, I knew would be too much."*

"For me, this boy being saved didn't make sense," Joe Cherokee continued. *"I'd never seen a man rescued from an attack. Especially on this lake, … especially at that moment in time. Cherokee gods saving non-native Americans just didn't happen. The* Yundwi Tsunsdi *and most of the other supernaturals in this cove would applaud the drowning, not make any effort to save your kind. Don't take offense."*

"When your people migrated into our mountains, most didn't care to share the land with "the savages" that called this area home. They steadily crowded them out, with the forced expatriation of the Cherokee a result. It was intolerably sad for the 'little people'. Their role as caretakers of the environment was overwhelmed as balance and sustainability were not yet in most colonist's vocabulary. Decades later in these mountains, the clear-cutting of the Appalachian forests was horrific for them, a near-apocalyptic experience. The Yundwi Tsunsdi *grew alienated. Many refused to make any attempt to continue their stewardship of man as related to the natural world."*

"To get an explanation about why your grandfather was rescued, I had to contact my Yundwi Tsunsdi *neighbors, the ones smiling up at you now. Interviewing those who would talk, and listening to other beings not in this clan, I realized there was something special going on. The 'little people' saw your grandfather as an* Asgaya, *a 'human being' in the best sense, someone who showed respect for the forest and this particular cove. They felt he might be someone they could instruct like the native-American Indians before him. The clan around us now gave the order to save him."*

"The 'little people' reached out to the Nunne'hi. *Neither ghosts nor gods, their Indian name means "the Immortals." They are compassionate to mankind, asking Indians into their lodge if they were freezing or hungry.* Nunne'hi *were fun-loving, showing up as Cherokee women to dances, disappearing into the night, into the rivers afterwards. Usually invisible to man, the* Nunne'hi *would appear in human form when the Cherokee people were threatened, helping them in times of war. Enlisting these supernaturals to help protect your Pop was a natural extension of their role in our world."*

"If I knew then what I know now, the young man I was dealing with decades ago, I would have re-introduced myself to your Pop the next day quoting Solzhenitsyn." Mr. Joe looked at grandfather and winked, because Russian literature was something the old man had force-fed him during their many years together. *"I would have told him that* "the Universe has

as many different centers as there are living beings in it." *Although I doubt even Aleksander knew how encompassing his words were."*

"I wasn't aware of the Russian authors then," said a smirking Pop. "I was a kid, just beginning to enjoy reading. Books I liked then were "Dune" and "Lord of the Rings," same as my friends. If Joe quoted that to me today, I'd quote Solzhenitsyn back at him; *"Of course God is endlessly multidimensional so every religion that exists on Earth represents some face, some side of God."* When he and I first met, I wasn't very religious. My inclination was to regard people by their behavior, not theology. If I bothered to regard them at all. Being that way made it easier to eventually accept the truth."

Joe Cherokee resumed his tale. *"Jack, my life has been integrated with the supernatural. You and your grandfather weren't aware of how your world is affected by the gods until having your eyes opened here on this cove. I've been telling you stories of the 'little people' in preparation for this day. You question the Cherokee fables, the gods lacking in depth of explanation. But we've lived with them, interacted. Indians never had to prove they existed. It makes myths and backstories less necessary."*

"I'd lived with the 'little people' long enough to be able to predict their behavior. But their act of saving your grandfather in the hopes of accepting him into their confidence was a surprise, a reflection of the respect he'd already earned from them as a young man. It's an honor not many of your kind ever had."

"The 'Water Tribe' of the Nunne'hi *rescued your Pop from the lake,"* revealed Mr. Joe.

"It was only after learning the "why" behind the rescue that I went to see your grandfather that next day," Joe Cherokee continued. *"He and I talked, but I mostly listened as he recalled his near-drowning. He tried to make logical sense of the event, wondering if he'd gotten tangled in vines wrapped on a limb underwater, the gnarled end of a tree branch resembling a hand. He thought he must have over-reacted and rolled the wrong way, the action twisting the vegetation around him, pulling him under. Whatever happened, he knew he was lucky to have escaped."* Mr. Joe's eyes met Jack's, *saying "I could tell he wasn't satisfied with that explanation. Your Pop likes common sense answers. He's not comfortable not knowing."*

"He'd encountered the supernatural firsthand with no preparation. Anybody in that situation would have struggled making sense of it."

Joe Cherokee looked over at Pop, sharing the retelling of the day his innocence was lost. *"I know he wanted to seem sane to a stranger like me, not some nut telling people he was swept out of the water in a rainbow of lights. But your grandfather knew his story wasn't true. Looking at me, seeing my reaction to his explanation, your Pop suspected I had insights that might help him understand what happened in the cove the day before."*

"I could tell, just as I can with you, that he suspected knowing what happened would complicate his life and challenge his perceptions," Mr. Joe said sadly, wistfully. He fondly looked over at grandfather. *"Lucky for me, I could tell your Pop had the courage to want to know the truth, regardless of the consequences."*

"I asked if he was open-minded," Mr. Joe continued. *"He cocked his head to the side before he answered, just like you do when you're weighing your options, making up your mind."* Then he said *"We'll have to see…"*

"Over the following weeks I educated him about the supernatural, the inhabitants of the cove, and my own, unique history. I agreed with the 'little people' that your teenaged grandfather was a real Asgaya, *a real man, even at his young age. Then we talked about the creature that tried to pull him under,"* Mr. Joe went on. *"I recounted the history of 'the mistake' unintentionally created through the carelessness of the 'Rock Cave' tribe of the* Yundwi Tsunsdi *and their inappropriate interactions with me as a youth."*

"Mistake?" Jack asked. *"You mean the gnarly fingered thing with the prune-skinned fingers?"*

"Yes," said Pop. "Moonshine Bob."

"Herman's there, too," said Joe Cherokee. *"they're a problem."*

CHAPTER EIGHT

Jack showed up to camp well after "tick patrol." They were lucky he showed up at all. While he considered it insane to introduce sailing to young people with monsters lurking in the water, what could he do? Recommend cancelling class? Should he try and explain why it was a bad day to get in the water? You know, as opposed to yesterday. This morning's turn-your-world-upside-down introduction to the supernatural wasn't compatible with his job keeping the summer camp experience carefree and fun for the kids.

As he was leaving the house, Jack caught himself looking at his grandfather's reflection in the kitchen window. He wasn't ready yet to look him in the eyes. Learning the reality of "Moonshine Bob" wasn't a welcome piece of information. He wasn't ready to join his grandfather in protecting the family from what everybody else thought was a tired joke. From the outside, it would look like he was joining his grandfather chasing windmills, Sancho Panza to Pop's Don Quixote, both deluded in their imaginary quest to be heroes.

Back in the moment, Jack "cowboyed up," reminded that the camp hadn't had a tragedy in years, the demons down there the whole time.

His first sail of the afternoon went well, the predicted wind indeed gentle and constant. With such ideal conditions, Jack was able to teach the kids both tacking into the wind and running with the wind safely. The next kids in line watched with interest and managed to learn the basics quickly. The "skippers in training" were so focused that Jack wondered if they were picking up on his fear and the seriousness of the day. Did they sense he equated swamping the boat with being swallowed by a lake monster? Of course not.

When Jack gathered enough courage to look over the port side of the sailboat to search the waters below, he saw no-longer-invisible *Nunne'hi*, the 'Water Tribe' smiling up at him. 'Moonshine Bob' and 'Herman' were nowhere to be found. The supernatural convoy insulating his kids from danger calmed him down, let him relax. He even smiled as the lessons came to an end and the last camper beached as he raised the boat's retractable wooden keel.

Once the kids saw Jack loosen up, they went wild, diving in to chase Mallards that paddled into the wrong cove. "Quack, quack, …, quack" they protested, easily frustrating their pursuers.

After the sailing lessons proved uneventful, Jack remembered another axiom from Pop. *"Fear is a handy servant, but a dangerous master."* He knew a lot of people are gripped in near-constant fear. Sadly, many are afraid of threats that are only hypothetical. Others are fearful of threats that are irrational, factually unreasonable, or even known to be false. Jack wondered how people governed by an imagined "dangerous master" of hypothetical or false threats would react to what he'd seen today.

Taking down the sails, securing the rigging, and storing the lightweight sailboats, Jack thought about his many years at the lake. Uneventful years. There was a reason no one took Pop seriously when he warned about 'Moonshine Bob' and 'Herman'. He kept them oblivious to the threat while Joe Cherokee, the 'little people', and the *Nunne'hi* managed the problem. They kept grandfather's family blissfully unaware, thinking the lake was safe. Eden's Creek Cove was ground zero in the battle of malicious enemies and their supernatural protectors, and nobody knew. Except Pop.

And now him. He'd been brought into the loop. The old guy's grandson, accepted by the 'little people', now responsible for the safety of the family, was next in line for the resulting ulcers and self-immolation of respect from those that had no clue.

This morning, Jack learned there are bigger problems than long-distance, disappointed girlfriends. He was expected to suddenly grow up and assume the mantle of fighter and protector. Given his powerful allies, Jack hoped his side had the upper hand. He'd have to face fear and trust that the *Yundwi Tsunsdi* would assist him as they helped his grandfather. So much for avoiding the oncoming storm of becoming a responsible adult. Now, with stinging rain hitting his face, winds buffeting against his body, he wondered why he hadn't seen the signs by the road outlining evacuation routes before.

In the spirit of not giving in, Jack decided to stick to his training schedule. When he got back to the lake house it would be like every other day. Everything would be OK. Only now he wasn't oblivious to the risks.

Things weren't OK further up the lake in the "narrows." 'Moonshine Bob' was up to no good. A slalom skier, hands-tired and arms-sore, was cradling the tow rope handle inside his bent elbow, coasting in the middle of the boat's draft to get a second wind before his next run. 'Bob' was waiting further up the lake near the shore, eyes poking just above the surface under the cover of branches from overhanging rhododendron. The captain of the ski boat followed the winding, narrow lake around a bend, turning into the sun. The glare off the water blinded him as he towed his no-longer-slaloming brother.

As the boat approached, 'Bob' took advantage of the driver's poor visibility. He'd pushed a water-logged section of a floating, mostly submerged oak tree trunk into the Mastercraft's path, swimming back to the cover of the underbrush to witness his scheme in action. The ski-boat and hazard met with a "thunk," the collision spectacular. The teen-aged captain flew headfirst out of the speeding, now driverless boat, splashing into the lake. Seeing his brother in the water, the skier let go of his ski rope, glided, and sank down next to him. The surprised driver was working hard to stay afloat, clothes soaked and heavy, wearing no safety vest.

Treading water together, the stunned boys were unharmed. But those who saw the crash from the nearby boat docks knew they wouldn't be safe for long. The freshly unmanned boat was circling around, moving right back towards them. Screaming teenaged girls alerted the boys to the threat. The craft just missed on its initial pass, the arc of its path too close for comfort, with its port side riding high over the swimmers. The craft's low-riding stern ground out a giant wave that crashed over them, the first of what looked to be several concentric orbits and close calls to come.

A quick-thinking, perhaps overly heroic dock owner assessed the problem. He quickly started up and pulled his larger Malibu VL-X out of its mooring. He accelerated directly towards the nightmare, steering his boat straight into the path of the oncoming vessel. He hit a glancing blow, his starboard side against the Mastercraft 190's starboard side, knocking it off course. The driverless boat crashed onto shore, wedging between boulders, bow up, engine grinding, and stern taking in water. Cheers erupted from the relieved onlookers.

The boys saved, the quick-thinking "hero" with his barely nicked-up boat got an earful from his terrified wife. 'Moonshine Bob' sunk underwater, dejected but smiling at his villiany.

Back home after camp, Jack prepared for his swim, unaware of the happenings just a couple of miles away. Shaking his head and laughing to himself, he thought of the saying "Ignorance is bliss." There couldn't have been a more appropriate aphorism for his life before this morning's great unveiling. He remembered a sarcastic comedian saying that if you're happy or content, you're obviously not paying attention. Well, …, Jack was paying attention.

Joe Cherokee stopped Jack at the door before he went down to the dock. *"I'll bet you'll swim faster today,"* he said, winking. *"I'm glad you're training. Your grandfather reacted the same way, with the same spirit. When he weighed the risks versus the joy the lake represented for him, he chose to fight, too."*

"I love to swim, Mr. Joe," Jack replied. "After what I heard this morning, I'm also trusting you and the *Nunne'hi* will continue doing what you've done successfully for so long. But there's something else running around my head. It tells me if I stop swimming they win. It's a feeling I get, thinking that when fear wins, 'Moonshine Bob' and 'Herman' get stronger."

Jack paused, thinking. He frowned, sighed, and rolled his eyes. Then he looked back at Joe Cherokee. "On the other hand, my head also thinks I made that up to feel better about doing something stupid. It's saying swimming now is something only a reckless kid would do. As Pop would say, "Reckless kid, but I repeat myself."

"Trust your gut," Mr. Joe replied. *"What you said isn't far from the truth. 'Herman', the monster Shoggoth 'Moonshine Bob' uses to carry out his dark desires, is a Nun'Yunu'Wi. In Cherokee lore, it is a water monster that responds to malevolent thoughts. The evil in people that drives them to harm others is the "on- switch" that awakens the beast, calling it into action."*

"Our drowned moonshiner first discovered 'Herman' inadvertently. As his frustration mounted - finding himself doomed to a life underwater, the threat of drowning a lifelong panic switch until his aquatic transformation - his thinking became ever more sinister, more evil. The Nun'yunu'Wi had been lying motionless in the deep waters of Lake Rabun for years, essentially dormant. It was called to action by evil thoughts from 'Moonshine Bob', anger and rage infiltrating all the way to the far corners of the lake."

"With each task that 'Herman' successfully completes, each malignant action that 'Bob' directs him to perform, it gets bigger," Mr. Joe explained. *"The more massive it grows, the harder the two demons are to defeat. 'Old Moonshine' looks over at his 'pet' these days and feels nearly invincible."*

"What do you mean when you say that 'Moonshine Bob' became trapped underwater?" Jack asked.

"'Moonshine' was once a mortal man," Mr. Joe revealed. *"That's why he looks like he does, clothed in torn, rotting overalls. He was just a young moonshiner, unlucky in life. He morphed into what he is today by chance, unfortunate serendipity, unlucky even in supernatural intervention."*

"'Moonshine Bob's' transformation couldn't have happened without my history with the Yundwi Tsunsdi," Mr. Joe continued. *"Without meaning to, the 'little people' are culpable for his creation. Without the 'little people' taking me under their wing as a child, without their unexplainable inability to get rid of the young moonshiner at their first encounter, he would have died of natural causes many years ago. He's our problem to solve and the reason the* Yundwi Tsunsdi *haven't left to join their supernatural brothers in migration."*

"What migration?" Jack inquired.

Mr. Joe continued. *"Every few centuries the* Yundwi Tsunsdi *and the*

Nunne'hi *in these mountains migrate deep into the Earth to renew their connection with our world. The expatriation of the Cherokee confirmed their suspicions of the colonizers and amplified their bias. They thought the surface world would soon to be ruined by occupiers they'd grown to despise.*

The forest stripped for lumber decades later confirmed their suspicions.

They made plans to move up their timetable, deciding to leave earlier, thinking they'd deal with the fallout after seeing what managed to survive. But those that inhabited Eden's Creek Cove had to delay their trek. There was the problem of an imbalance they'd created, a mistake now over a century old whose disposal couldn't be left to chance."

Pop joined them on the porch, anxious and barely able to look at his grandson. Shoulders slumped, head hung, he moved slowly to take his chair. "For years I've been worried that telling anybody about our cove and its combatants, especially a family member, would be too much for them to believe, too hard to wrap their head around," Pop said, looking back in his past. "It's been a heavy weight to carry. I hadn't realized how unloading the "truth bomb" that exploded all over you this morning would affect me. Thinking sharing the truth might set me free, instead it's made the weight heavier."

"Jack, I know you roll your eyes at my "Deep Thoughts,"" Pop began, fingers doing "air quotes" around the last two words. "It's not just me trying to teach you. It's a way to let you into my head. Imagine how I struggle with what you've seen. You know how I like to know the answers to the world's big questions, as much as they're knowable. Then imagine having to make decisions you never, ever thought you'd need to make, protecting the people you love from things you will never understand, living in a world of supernatural beings you didn't know existed."

After a deep breath, Pop mined his archetype-dominated brain and kept explaining. "I've thought long and hard about what not sharing my secret reveals about me. What I've learned is another "Deep Thought." The existence of evil challenges us. It makes us decide. I think God's gift to mankind is "freedom of choice" in the context of recognizing good and evil. How we react to the evil we experience in our lives, the choices we make, defines us. The person we build from our decisions give us an opportunity to glorify Him, our Creator."

"Without darkness, there is no light. Without evil you can't recognize goodness. Making choices, responding to times in life when things aren't going well, is how we gain character. Like I've told you before, it's how we acquire the wisdom and courage to become the people we were meant to be. You don't grow, you don't learn, if never challenged by the bad, the unexpected, or even the … uh, …, supernatural."

"This morning, I was forced to confront the fact that I've made bad choices, especially thinking I could shield everyone, make the lake a vacation from worry by myself. But I've watched, helpless, as 'Herman' continues to grow. It makes me feel …, incapable. I've been hiding the supernatural from you from the perspective of fear. God gives me the choice to be honest out of love. Telling you the truth, letting you into the fight, let's me share that love, trust that God is in charge, not me."

"It's my pride," continued grandfather. "I learned it's wrong to think I could, or should, shoulder the burden without family support. It was me wanting to be the hero, prove I could figure it out with Mr. Joe and friends, not wanting to admit I was failing. I've always tried to explain things using facts and logic. God reminds me that faith is not about reason. It is about trust."

Pop unbowed his head and looked to Jack, eyes sad, as if asking forgiveness.

Joe Cherokee spoke up, breaking the brief silence. *"It's been painful waiting on your grandfather to grow in his understanding of the Great Spirit, Unetlanvhi."*

Grandfather shot a surprised look his way, realizing only now the Indian knew he'd chosen the wrong path these many years. Allowing him space, not lecturing him about his bad choices, learn without being told, …, how "inconsiderate" of him. The corner of Pop's mouth twisted into a half grin.

"Everyone knows you're a self-righteous know-it-all," Joe Cherokee laughed. *"Self-reliant, intelligent people are often the hardest to learn the truth. There's a Bible story in the Gospel of Mark about Jesus in the wilderness. He spent 40 days and 40 nights being tempted by Satan. Finally, the Holy Spirit descended upon him, showing him the Truth. Your grandfather knew this story and taught it to me, but I guess it took a while to understand*

how it reflected on him."

"Your history's not perfect either, Joe," Pop countered. "I remember you trying several days in a sweat lodge with mushrooms and herbs, thinking it might cook you into wisdom. Through that, you understood how, when you were young, the *Yundwi Tsunsdi* were complicit in a similar deception. They allowed you to go down one rabbit hole after another, searching for explanations for bad things that happened, trying to fix things broken by fate, all the while knowing you were just banging your head against a wall."

"It's better being on this end, watching you struggle," said Joe. *"That's been as entertaining to me as I must have been for the 'little people'."*

"The idea of mushrooms in a sweat lodge was a prescription from a tribal medicine man. That experience re-introduced me to 'Ocasta', our Cherokee god of knowledge. 'Ocasta' creates chaos one day and instills order and structure the next. He changed my personal definition of what's fair. Psilocybin, the active ingredient in mushrooms, broke down my defenses, allowed me to experience "The Great Light.""

Joe Cherokee paused; *'Like your grandfather, I learned the "let go, let God" message. We both call it revelation, the acceptance of the 'Great Spirit'. To me, he is* Unetlanvhi, *to you an your grandfather, he is Jehovah. In knowing him, we lose the fear of death, knowing he has great plans for us."*

Jack listened through the men's "Deep Thoughts," amazed at his own patience. Tempted to roll his eyes, he felt compassion instead. The two old schemers with secrets, one a curmudgeon, the other a relic of a past culture, seemed more vulnerable to him. He was understanding more about how much Pop's secret played into their interactions all these years.

Jack thought back to times he was dropped off at the lake by himself with both grandparents. After a long day swimming, they'd tuck him in with a book at bedtime. "Pinocchio" was a favorite. After a day spent with morning walks in the woods, he'd be expected to tell them what he found. He explored the rock grottos by the creek, skipping stones and hunting crawfish. Pop swam unobtrusively close by while he learned to swim without "floaties" or a vest.

"Pinocchio" thought Jack. He recognized his grandparents were raising him to be a "real boy," what Joe Cherokee called an *Asgaya*. Pop challenged him to jump off the second story deck. He helped him put on goggles and find things that sank to the bottom. 'Grams' put him in a kayak. But what she did most often was ask him to make choices, reminding him "to let conscience be my guide." They would see the stars at night, 'Grams' showing him the constellations on her "SkyView" phone app. If there was a star that piqued his interest, she would ask if there was anything he wanted. She held her finger to her lips and said if he wish upon a star, silently, his desire was more likely to come true.

It was all so transparent, Jack realized. Pop was 'Geppetto', 'Grams' was "the Blue Fairy." Throw in Joe Cherokee as 'Jiminy Cricket' and it all came together. Remembering times where - just like Pinocchio, like all boys, like all of humanity - he'd get caught in a lie, he'd see them shake their heads. "Your nose is growing," they'd laugh. Jack swore he'd literally see it happen, too. They wouldn't let him get away with it. They'd wait for the truth to come out and love him through it.

As a teenager, when given a chore, Jack would find a way to escape. He'd play with the rich kids on the lake whose parents gave them everything they wanted. Just like the runaways taken to the circus in the fable, Jack could imagine them turning into donkeys. Going back home, the chore still unfinished, 'Grams' would meet him and stay there keeping him company until he finished, even if it got dark.

Jack would explore every bad idea rather than letting his conscious be his guide. And how did the book end? He'd forgotten. Jack knew it had something to do with "coming of age" in a symbolic kind of way. Pop may have even said there was a reason Jiminy Cricket's initials were J.C. and his advice was to "always let your conscience be your guide." Jack wondered if he'd purposely put it out of his mind.

The two old men patiently waited as Jack daydreamed.

"I hope whatever happens doesn't end up with me in the belly of a whale," Jack said to the consternation of grandfather and Mr. Joe. He waited for a response. Not getting one, he realized his Pinocchio analogy hadn't been shared, a completely missed connection.

"That's a flippant comment to make," Mr. Joe said. *"You know that 'Her-*

man's' no joke, right?"

Changing the subject, hoping he didn't anticipate his fate, Jack said "I'd like to know more about Mr. Joe's past. The more I hear, the more confused I get."

"I'll tell you about my relationship with the Yundwi Tsundi *when you finish your training,"* Joe replied. *"Maybe even let you know how 'Moonshine Bob' came into the picture,"* Joe Cherokee said, handing Jack his robe. *"But first you should train."*

Jack swam. He didn't end up 'Herman's dinner. His time was fast. "So that's what motivated Pop," he said to himself. "I'll have to ask how he conjured 'Herman' chasing him in a collegiate racing pool."

CHAPTER NINE

"To begin, Jack, you must have guessed from our conversations that I am far older than you were aware," Mr. Joe began, jumpstarting his biography after Jack's swim. The dinner table had 'Gram's' meatloaf recipe and Pop's garlic mashed potatoes and southern green beans, all disappearing before the Indian's eyes.

"I was born a Cherokee, growing up here along the Tallulah River. Our villages were on the tributary creeks scattered throughout the valleys between the mountains. We farmed corn, squash, sweet potatoes, sunflower, and beans. We fished the rivers and hunted deer, small game, and turkey. We gathered berries at the edge of the trees and chestnut in the forest. The Creek Indian Tribe was close enough that we didn't wander too many days south or east of our lands."

"Cherokee, like other native Americans, had our numbers decimated by the smallpox virus, something the Spanish brought to the continent centuries before. While struggling to recover from that horror, every new contact with the 'Old World' *invaders resulted in another plague for which we had no defense,"* Mr. Joe continued, voice flat, his eyes closed in the memory. *"Measles, typhus, cholera, and swine flu killed countless Indians. Whole com-*

munities were wiped out. Great cities were abandoned because of the "germ warfare" and never repopulated. Disease dropped our number so severely that it was difficult to farm, feed the survivors, or put up stores for the winter. Trade contracted as fewer goods were made."

"As our strength waned, our society was pushed backwards to a more tribal, subsistence level. We were no match for the Europeans, especially with their weapons and technology. Settlers were moving in, brazenly declaring our best lands were theirs. They had guns to back up their claims. Hope for our culture surviving was low."

"The allure of mysticism grew as our efforts to survive the occupation were failing," Mr. Joe continued. "The Cherokee had always coexisted with the supernatural, but our interactions mainly involved acknowledgement and offerings. We wished for good weather at planting season, luck with a hunt, or suggestions of names for our children. Our default position with the gods was simple. Don't do things that prompted them to punish you. They weren't expected to be reliably transactional in our dealings with men."

"With our way of life disappearing around us, we asked more from our medicine men and mystics instead," Joe Cherokee explained. "It was through them we approached our gods. We knew the importance the gods placed on balance, working with, not against, the natural world. We thought they'd not only judge but punish the Europeans, hoping they'd fight them directly. We assumed the Cherokee were the preferred stewards of the world."

"I had a twin brother," Mr. Joe continued, visibly saddened by the memory. "We couldn't have been closer. Even at a very young age, we knew the concerns of our people. Thinking ourselves powerful, at least in our imaginations, we decided to ask the gods for help. The rock grottos around the creeks were known to be their home, and we were fortunate to find and be embraced by the Yundwi Tsunsdi."

"At the time, my brother and I didn't know why the 'little people' tolerated us hanging around them, much less joining them in play. We were children and didn't care. We just knew that they were our gods, not the God of the invaders." Joe Cherokee looked down and sighed. "We'd heard stories of the Nunne'hi and how they were known to fight with us against our enemies, appearing suddenly from their usual invisibility outfitted in golden armor. We knew they couldn't be killed. We hoped having them on our side would be *enough. But help from the 'little people' could be useful as well."*

"As it turned out, the gods chose to play a less active role than we'd hoped," Mr. Joe explained. *"Much later in life I learned the 'little people' allowed us so close because of a fascination they had for twin children. My brother and I were merely a curiosity. They never intended to intervene on our side because of our interactions. The* Nunne'hi, *who decades later brought some of our Cherokee tribe in a high mountain cave to hide them from US soldiers, didn't fight, either."*

"The tale of my time with the Yundwi Tsunsdi *is long and layered with many twists and turns. The 'little people' have a unique ability to share history. It's a means to chronicle time, as if looking through a window into the past."* Joe Cherokee smiled, knowing how Jack might respond to what would happen next. *"They are willing to transport you in time. They say that a picture is worth a thousand words. A movie, on the other hand, ..."*

The *Yundwi Tsunsdi* surrounded Jack where he had turned and leaned back against the kitchen island. They jumped onto the granite countertop, standing above and behind him, waving their hands above him. Soft chanting began as they bent forward, their long white hair forming a curtain surrounding his head. Jack fell unconscious, his body immobile. As closed eyes twitched under their lids, an induced dream state began. A quick synopsis of the life of Joe Cherokee and the 'little people' was the 'movie reel' underway.

Jack's vision began with the familiar view of the mountains surrounding the family cove. Eden Creek he recognized, but Lake Rabun wasn't there. Instead, there was the roar of a turbulent river coming from deep down the canyon. Below, he could see a pair of identical black-haired boys, each wearing short buckskin breeches. They were playing on a rock outcropping over the creek that wound down to the river. The boys disappeared in and out of the surrounding thickets of rhododendron and mountain laurel, vigorously searching for something. As their efforts proved fruitless and the day wore on, they gave up and went back home.

Time elapsed until the twin brothers finally found the Yundwi Tsunsdi. *Then the pair were allowed to get close, interacting with the small, longhaired inhabitants of the stone grottos. He saw the two boys exploring the creeks and rivers, never apart, always near the company of their supernatural friends.*

Jack noticed the 'little people' couldn't stop giggling and pointing at the mirror-image children and their antics, nothing like the attitude Mr. Joe described in his stories.

Once a little older, the two boys were seen to have insinuated themselves into the daily lives of the 'little people'. When the twins were alone, Jack could hear their youthful voices. Even without knowing their language, he could tell they spoke like conspirators plotting.

After one of these animated conversations, they both ran over to a cache of the Yundwi Tsunsdi, *bowed their heads and averted their eyes. They pleaded with their "friends." Somehow he understood them as they described how the Cherokee were being overrun by the Europeans. Something had to be done. They were sure to repel the invaders if they just had the help of their gods.*

The 'little people' shook their heads. Nothing changed.

Jack witnessed the twin's frustration. The boys didn't know what to do. He could see one of the brothers come up with a plan, vigorously gesturing and excited. He'd tell his twin they should try and steal magic from the Yundwi Tsunsdi, *take things they refused to share, and give it to warriors to fight the settlers.*

The twins spent lots of time observing the powerful waters of the Tallulah River. They admired how the Yundwi Tsunsdi *fearlessly went into and out of the turbulent currents. Both boys had been warned by their family of the river's danger, in their minds a place only safe for the gods. The more adventurous brother, a daredevil of a boy, thought he could use this knowledge. He predicted that the 'little people' would save him if he "accidentally" slipped into the currents. Even with the risk involved, they thought they'd try it. The brothers planned to take advantage of the 'little people's' compassion by stealing a rescue spell or a healing potion.*

But tricksters like the 'little people' weren't naïve. A heavy branch pulled the drowning boy out of the river before he even gulped any water. Tricking tricksters proved to be a challenge. They teased the boys, pretending to fall for their games before laughing as they held back the knowledge of magic the desired. They would then play jokes on the twins for amusement. One brother might see his hand transformed into a crawfish claw. The other would appear to grow a crow's beak. Neither could tell if it was an illusion or reality. Either way it would "clear up" by the end of the day.

After a lot of effort by the boys, they were taught some elementary magic. The first spell shared with the twins was an incantation to make them invisible to people wandering into the grottos. Another was to silence any sounds they made, making their area quiet to passersby.

Magic like this would have helped the Cherokee in their fight against the colonists, besides shocking the medicine men of their village. But the twins only learned how to make themselves invisible and quiet, the magic only working around the 'little people's' grotto, nowhere else. Worst of all, they couldn't figure out a way to teach the skills to the warriors of their tribe. They needed more.

But progress came slowly. Pleading with their supernatural friends to teach them, constantly nagging, the 'little people' responded by allowing the twins insight into the talents different creatures possessed. The next spells involved the animal inhabitants of the forest and creeks. The boys learned that adapting each animal's unique survival skills for their personal use was possible. Acquiring these skills was interesting, exciting, and fun. But the knowledge remained limited to the grotto, again difficult to translate for use by others.

Armed with powers no child could imagine, the hijinks of the daring brother often irritated and alienated the Yundwi Tsunsdi. *The 'little people's' patience tested, they shunned the boy for long periods of time. His rule-breaking and resulting abandonments led him to take ever greater risks. Successes he had transferring "creature powers" for his own use made him feel chosen by the spirits of the forest for greater things. He imagined he might climb trees, jump off, and glide down like a flying squirrel. Or he'd burrow into the lake floor and live underwater like a turtle. Surely his magical abilities would be welcomed by his tribe and prove useful in battle, even though he was still quite small.*

One day the predictable happened. The boy used a spell involving the Hellbender salamander, an ancient amphibian with unique air-exchange capabilities. Thinking himself magically immune from drowning, and not wanting to lose his nerve and surface before giving it a good try, he weighed himself down with stones in a natural pool near the secret grotto. Meaning to force himself to master underwater breathing, he drowned instead. His twin brother found him and pulled him up the bank, banging on his chest and blowing air into his mouth like he'd seen Medicine men do. But it was too late. Even the Yundwi Tsunsdi *couldn't bring him back.*

The surviving brother was inconsolable. He couldn't imagine the remainder of his life without his brother by his side. Certainly, he knew he couldn't go back home without him, trying to face his parents alone. He imagined the despair and disappointment on their faces. They would ask why he hadn't kept his brother safe and alive.

After not coming home for days, the village went out to look for the boys. People were aware they spent their days near the big river and feared the worst. They couldn't have known the surviving brother didn't want to be found. He hid, cloaked invisibly in the thick underbrush with his sobbing quieted, using spells he'd learned to escape detection. Even the anguished calls of his mother didn't lure him out of his hiding, his guilt about his brother's death so heavy in his heart.

In a long period of grief and loneliness the boy found a justification for living. Something grand enough to honor his brother's memory. A reason to stay alive that made sense and gave him purpose. He decided to dedicate his life to excelling in the talent his brother was attempting to acquire. Specifically, he would learn to use the 'little people's' magic spells to protect people from drowning.

Jack saw visions of the surviving boy becoming a teenage Joe Cherokee. He witnessed the young Joe working late into the night countless times in his hidden cave by the creek. Joe continued to persuade the Yundwi Tsundi *to assist him with different potions and incantations. The supernaturals didn't share their magic as a rule, but pity for the lone remaining twin made them generous.*

More time went by, with puffs of powdery smoke illuminated by rainbow-colored lights rising between the trees evidence of his ongoing experiments. Jack witnessed salamanders, crawfish, turtles, and frogs being captured and studied. Failed trials on rabbits and squirrels left them soaked and lifeless, all the while with the empathetic 'little people' steadily sharing more magic than they should with their heartbroken houseguest.

Slowly and steadily, Joe Cherokee made progress, but never enough to accomplish his goal. The memory of his brother drove him, their separation his first conscious thought in the morning and the last thing on his mind before sleep. The quest to honor his twin wouldn't let him stop.

But the loneliness of being away from the company of people eventually proved difficult to ignore. More importantly, Joe began to think it was inappropriate for a human being to use the supernatural to cheat death. He noticed the Yundwi Tsunsdi *treated him with increasing concern, realizing the threat his experiments posed to the balance of nature. Joe could feel the wrongness of it, too. He could see the cycle of human life was a beautiful thing. Messing with it cheapened it in a way.*

Cherokee Joe, now a young man, made the decision to stop trying. He parted friends with the 'little people', both sides admitting it was for the best, a good time to pursue a new destiny.

Coming out of his self-imposed exile, Joe learned he had been gone for several decades, displaced in time. This was true for many who lingered with the Yundwi Tsundi *and then tried to go back to their lives. Jack saw Joe leave the cave and the creekside to a much different world. The bulk of the Cherokee nation had been gathered up and marched to reservations in the Midwest, a great many dying along the way. The dreadful journey had been named "the Trail of Tears," with much of the indian culture forced out of the mountains as well. His family was gone, as was his village.*

There were Indians who were able to remain by choice, having assimilated with the homesteaders. They joined Cherokee hidden by the Nunne'hi, *a group less inclined to give up their culture. When the buckskin-clad Joe encountered them, he was ridiculed as primitive. Unsurprisingly, nobody recognized him. Examining their faces, Joe imagined he could place a few of them as friends from childhood, but they had grown quite old. The time Joe spent with the supernaturals made him barely age by comparison.*

Gold had been discovered in the mountains of North Georgia. The resulting "rush" of miners brought in all manner of people hoping to strike it rich. With the Indians forced out, the land with its many gold-sprinkled rivers and creeks was wide open for claims. Jack witnessed Mr. Joe deciding to join the diverse collection of rough men. When with them, panning for gold in his treasured Appalachian waters, he did what he could to honor the Yundwi Tsunsdi *and their focus on taking what is just necessary. He tried to keep the miner's footprint light and the creeks and rivers alive.*

Men being men, they left destruction in their wake. The "Little People" mourned.

CHAPTER TEN

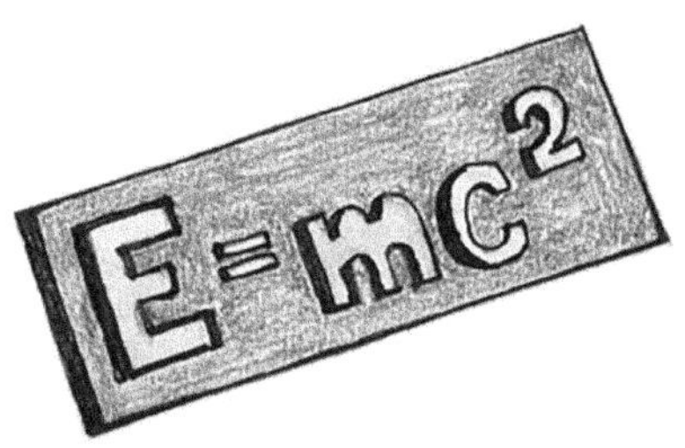

Jack awakened after "Joe Cherokee, His Early Life" concluded, a documentary produced by supernatural videographers, as the hypnotism came to an end.

"How was your trip?" the Indian asked, anxious to hear what he'd learned. *"Your Pop and I are anxious to know."*

"A lot to take in, Mr. Joe," Jack said, wrapping his head around the thought that his grandfather's buddy was working into his third century. "I suppose if Cherokee mini-gods are sharing home movies with me, believing you're older than "the Star-Spangled Banner" should come as no surprise." Jack looked at Mr. Joe with sadness. "I'm sorry about your twin brother, man. That's a hard thing, I imagine."

"Did you get to 'Moonshine Bob'?" Pop asked, too anxious to wait for Joe Cherokee to reply.

"No," Jack replied to his grandfather. "Most of what I saw was before *"the War of Northern Aggression."*"

"What?" Mr. Joe asked, perplexed.

"That's what Pop called the American Civil War," Jack said. "He'd heard it called that by grandparents of friends he grew up with, folks descended from the "Old South," who thought they were noble martyrs to a supposed grand cause, their drawls lamenting "tha Wahwah o Knowthun Aggreshun.""

"Oh. Bad times." Mr. Joe recalled. *"Lots of people around here died. One out of three men didn't live through the war from this region. That's what the newspaper said. It seemed worse than that. The men not coming home left many of their families starving in their absence. Bad times went on for years, well after the shooting ended."*

"Sorry about your people, too, Mr. Joe," Jack made sure to say.

"Thank you, Jack. Coming back to the times just after the "Trail of Tears," hearing about the cruelty of the circumstances, was horribly sad," Joe Cherokee replied. *"As was the loss of my brother so long before. Just know, after so many years, I've learned to appreciate peace, keeping my focus on looking for harmony between men. I've come to understand that it's not just the Cherokee that are my people. People are my people."* His B-movie accent returned. "Even you paleface girly men."

Jack smiled at the put down, the funny accent, and the break from serious memories.

"I've thought a lot about this, as you might expect given my age. Too often, unfair things happen to the most innocent among us," Mr. Joe went on. *"It offends our sense of justice. Life is so morally random. When my brother died, I was depressed for far too long. I isolated from family. Staying in that place stagnates the soul. It wastes your life. It's an affront to the Great Spirit,* Unetlanvhi."

"When I came out of the worst of it, I spent years mad about the unfairness," Joe Cherokee continued. *"I channeled my anger, choosing to use that energy for a higher purpose. My twin brother's death inspired me, thinking I might be able to stop what happened to him from happening to others. But I learned this is like declaring war against life itself. Life is injustice. Innocents die. Sometimes, like your grandfather reminds us, the pricks and the assholes win. You can lose everything overnight to something as mindless and random as a storm, much less from illness and foreign invasion like the Cherokee did."*

"Politicians use people's rage against injustice to get power," Pop interjected, unable to let this teaching moment pass. "They'll earnestly stand there, promising they'll fix the inequities between people, make things fair. But this inevitably destroys freedom and stokes envy. Changing who is in power by promising equality of outcomes in life just changes the oppressor. It unfailingly ends up fostering a culture of death. Like Solzenitsyn says, *the line of evil runs through every human heart.*" They may have admirable objectives at the beginning. But they learn early on that promises give them power. And, no matter how counter the results of their policies are to the results they desired, they promise more of the same. Power corrupts."

Jack and Joe Cherokee looked at each other and rolled their eyes. Pop and his politics. They were used to the old guy interrupting, but it didn't keep them from groaning when he did.

"I've chosen another way to deal with the seemingly mean aspects of life, the hard parts of living in the Great Spirit's creation," Joe Cherokee continued, picking up where he left off. *"I acknowledge that life is not fair and never will be. I accept that bad things happen that are out of my control. Through your Christian God I've learned that no matter the situation, I should do everything I can to live a life of purpose and gratitude, loving the people that share the world, being there in times of grief to give support. Simply making room for the good by crowding out the bad honors Him."*

"Your grandfather and I recognize when a human element is causing suffering," Mr. Joe said, acknowledging Pop. *"Like most human beings, we have an innate ability to identify lies and recognize injustice. Our consciousness helps us see when an innocent is being wronged or respect isn't warranted. Your grandfather and I choose to stand up against those things, something that many choose to avoid. We feel it is our duty as men to help truth win."*

"Our consciousness is something we share with God, the best source of our nature," grandfather added. "It strives, seeks accomplishment, hungers for knowledge, and loves and protects our children. Without unfairness, tragedy, and wickedness there would be no opposites to champion. Our human consciousness allows us to reflect the goodness of God in our fight."

Pop couldn't help himself, continuing to unleash his insights, thinking them too important not to share with Jack. "God created us with varying amounts of talent, different capacities for work, and only the opinions of others to judge whether the value we provide has worth. And that's OK. Nations aren't equal in their foundational principles, resources, or the opportunities they foster. But it is from the inequities of the world that creativity, beauty, and progress arise."

"There is no fair distribution of genius. Think of the symphonies of Beethoven or Einstein's Theory of Relativity," he continued. "As for nations, out of the oppressive, morally questionable colonization of the Americas came a constitutional government that defines all men as created equal. This foundational principle directly led to the Civil War that abolished slavery, slaveholding a sad fact of life for all human existence until that brother-against-brother conflict. Both tragedies, the American colonization and the Civil War, guided us towards the good, making dramatic improvements in our nation. In both cases, good people died fighting for backwards ideals. One of the ideals we support as healthy and forward-looking is equality of opportunity, not outcomes."

Pop felt he'd said enough, pausing and waiting for Jack's reply.

After an uncomfortably long time, Jack looked up. Then he looked over at his grandfather. The he looked over at Mr. Joe. It was obvious they expected an answer, and he was on the clock. Timidly, he turned again and said to his Pop; "Which brings us to 'Moonshine Bob'?"

Jack hoped his guess was correct. Still dazed from the 'little people's' visions of Joe Cherokee's earlier life, he wasn't listening to the 'old guy's' explanations and philosophies of life. He came clean. "Ya'll lost me at "stagnates the soul." The word 'Stagnate' made me think of the outhouses and soiled areas around Mr. Joe's goldminer's camp from my vision. Yuck."

The two old sages looked at each other and sighed.

"Sorry," Jack said. "Missed the whole "Deep Thoughts" thing again, didn't I?" The corner of his mouth raised again in a crooked smile. "Whoops." The mischievous glint in his eyes tickled his grandfather. The three burst out laughing.

They went out to the porch with the *Yundwi Tsunsdi* in tow. The night wasn't over, the dawn still hours away. It didn't take long for Jack to fall asleep, stretched out on the outdoor couch, drooling on the all-weather pillows. The still-awake conspirators decided to take advantage by introducing the history of 'Moonshine Bob' to Jack's dreams. Low chanting began. It was time to change biographic "movie reels," courtesy of the 'little people'.

CHAPTER ELEVEN

Jack watched as a derelict young man stumbled off the dirt road, exhausted after miles of ducking, running, and hiding. Heavy, dark rainclouds were blowing in over a mountain from the west. He looked over his shoulder to see if he was being followed. No one there, he jumped across the spillway and worked his way through thorns from wild blackberries towards the woods. Scratched and soaked, he hung his head before disappearing into a wall of rhododendrons.

Lawmen found his family still and Jack viewed them dynamiting it, the Rabun County sheriff's preferred message to anybody in the illegal trade of homemade spirits. From conversations heard, Jack knew they'd been making a show of it, "cracking down" so to speak, all to calm down the local church ladies. Big distillers needn't worry. Arrangements had been made. Inconsequential players suffered. It didn't take much to blow up the young man's operation. That done, they turned to the task of finding and jailing the moonshiner.

{The Yundwi Tsunsdi *then opened a wider window, allowing Jack to expe-*

rience the moonshiner's thoughts and recollections, their skill at mental telepathy shared with their new ally}.

Jack felt sorrow in the young man watching him reminisce. If they'd asked, the fugitive could have told them the still they demolished was already garbage, even before the lawmen turned it into rubble. Its moonshine was garbage, too. He hadn't maintained the fouled spring water intake, the boiler pot was filthy, and the whole system leaked because he didn't have flour to make paste to plug the holes. As for the mash, some of it came from other people's waste, usually discarded corn, rotting apples, or even potato peels animated by insects. Folks treated his product like poison.

Technically it was poison. While cooking, the young moonshiner rarely waited for the "head," the first, low boiling point condensate, to finish its discard before collecting the liquid in a jar. Methanol, the stuff that could make you blind, was there, with a bunch of other things not fit to drink. If it spilled, it killed the plants. He knew it might kill him, too. He didn't care. It made him high, and he wanted to get high right away.

He should be ashamed. His family name used to represent a quality product. But that was years ago.

His grandpappy learned to distill liquor in Ireland before the potato famine sent him packing. Emigrating to America, he settled in Rabun County. He'd heard it was known for loose rules for home distilling. Settling in, he took the job of constructing a good still seriously. He had a real copper swan neck coming off his mash pot, with a whiskey helmet to boot, distilling again what his prized "racoon pecker" spilled efficiently from the condenser. People appreciated the quality of his product, his good reputation well earned.

The family liquor business took a step further when his father took over. The Tallulah Falls Railroad opened a line up to the Tallulah River, with sightseers from Atlanta coming up to picnic or spend the night at one of the many comfortable Inns at the south rim of the awe-inspiring Tallulah Gorge. The Gorge and the Tallulah River – "The Niagara of the South" - were among the most popular tourist destinations in Georgia. Pappy's "shine" became a popular under-the-counter souvenir.

But liquor production, outlawed by the Union occupiers after the Civil War, was a complicated thing to do. Competitors could sabotage your still. The police could demand a cut of the profits, tearing it down if the extortion didn't *work. There were even conflicts with the God-fearing folks who kept High-lands, North Carolina "dry." Living just across the border, their children had no trouble buying liquor in Rabun. Highland's sheriffs travelled down the mountain, crossed the state line, arrested moonshiners, brought them back to their 4,000 feet-above-sea-level enclave, and threw them in jail. Famously, the resulting enmity erupted into a blockade of the town's only east-west connection by fellow Rabun County moonshiners.*

Jack felt resignation from the young man as he witnessed him remembering his family's past. The illegality of their business caught up with the family decades before. His grandpappy died from a combination of old age and heartbreak when the lawmen dismantled his still. His father found odd jobs at hotels along the canyon rim. One day he accidentally started a fire that burned the finest South Rim Inn down. The incident got him blackballed from the Gorge tourism industry as a result. When his mother died in childbirth, his defeated father gave up, the son that survived raised practically feral.

Grown to a teenager, the bored and hungry boy tried to make money the only way he knew how. He collected scattered remnants of past bootleg moonshine construction and tried to piece them together. He begged his father for assistance and managed to learn the basics of distillation. But once the first results of their shared home brewing finally dripped out, after the first purposeful work he and his hapless father had done together, his old man drank all they made. After time, with the only connection to his father being alcohol, the boy gave up and joined his father drinking himself into oblivion.

When his father died, the boy found odd jobs from old friends of his grandpappy. This made him enough to occasionally eat, but he spent most of his money on mash. But having mash rarely led to sales of his moonshine and spendable cash, given his proclivities.

And now he was on the run. Running even though he would eat better in jail and be able to get out of the weather. The rain, a constant companion in this famously wet county, was cold and drenching. Mud caked his worn boots. His head throbbed from last night's consumption of the only unbroken jar of moonshine he had left.

There was some good fortune, though. The week before he'd found a condenser blown into the woods from the explosion of a neighbor's still. It was all he took with him when fleeing from the law. And now, tripping and falling through heavy underbrush, another serendipitous thing happened. He found himself in a rock grotto with a cave, dry and hidden, just above a clear water creek. There was even a spring at its base. A chinquapin tree ripe with nuts, dropped and ready for eating, sealed the deal. Maybe his luck had changed, he thought, the crap-show of his miserable life finally turning around.

Unknown to him, he'd stumbled upon the home of the 'Rock Tribe' of the Yundwi Tsunsdi'. He curled up under a rock ledge out of the rain.

Days later, Jack could see that the 'little people' were none too happy to have a smelly, slow-witted drunk stumble into their home. Besides his fetid breath and fouled clothing, the snores erupting from his throat and gaping mouth could wake the dead. He'd crashed their cave a couple days earlier and showed no signs of leaving. In fact, he was scouting their quarters, stealing items from a nearby logging camp, and had prepared a routine place to sleep.

To make matters worse, the mind-games the Yundwi Tsunsdi *relied on when dealing intruders weren't working. The young squatter spent so much of his life just surviving, being the object of so little attention, so little affection, he had no issues with hardship. All he needed was enough for now. If he encountered problems, bigger problems were out there. The 'little people' were having a hard time scaring him off.*

Meanwhile, the broken-down man-on-the-run that stumbled into the camp of the 'little people' began to change. Living in the company of the supernaturals rubbed off a little vitality and strength each successive day. The gaunt, renegade hillbilly who found the hidden grotto steadily lost his sickly grey pallor and improved his stooped, limping gait. One day he almost smiled. Once. (Jack, seeing things unfold, wondered if the guy had forgotten how).

More unfortunate for the reluctant hosts, the squatter remained dimwitted, with maybe a touch of fetal alcohol syndrome, despite his physical improvement. The moonshiner's simple nature and uncalculating mind kept the 'little people' frustrated.

How else could the young man fail to notice the 'little people's' efforts to get him to leave? Invisible to his sight, they would trip him, sending him tumbling down the rocks. When he would gather firewood, if he turned his back, the cord of wood would be soaking wet. If he did manage to start a fire, it would be extinguished in a burst of dirt and dust.

How could he not have been suspicious when there were burrs in his bed, sharp bits of broken pottery strewn across the floor, and squirrel scat mixed in with gathered food? Thorny vines would greet him in the morning covering the entrance to the cave. His few clothes would be missing, his shirt later found buried in leaves, pants tangled in a high branch over the creek.

Anyone else would have been suspicious. Anyone would have had concerns.

Not him. He didn't think about it, not much for analysis. Things had improved so much for the moonshiner that he looked past the irritations, not dwelling on their cause. Any misfortune that he unknowingly experienced at the hands of the vexed Yundwi Tunsdi *was dramatically overshadowed by how fortunate his new surroundings proved to be.*

That first day on the run, climbing the new grotto, he dropped his condenser, watching helplessly as it banged noisily down the rocks. He reflexively cursed loudly as it fell. Looking up, sure he had given away his position, knowing he was caught, he watched as the lawmen walked right by as if nothing had happened. Later, cold from the rain, he tempted fate again by making a fire. Even with wet wood and the resulting thick smoke, nobody came to investigate.

Over time he confirmed no one could see inside the grotto. There was some type of a visual barrier blocking the site from the outside world. Besides invisibility, any sounds he made, no matter how loud, couldn't be heard either.

Magic, he thought. Maybe grandpappy's tales of enchanted spaces inhabited by leprechauns were true. He hoped so. He'd sure like to meet one. Maybe he'd even get a chance to raid their pot-o-gold. But where would he spend it? He was an outlaw, a fugitive. They'd throw him in jail if he left. And they'd take his leprechaun treasure.

He stole from everywhere. Anything not nailed down he took, stealing from all around his encampment. The authorities suspected the thefts were from a criminal newly arrived, triangulating the probable location of the thief from places items were taken. But they walked all around his invisible hideout having no clue he was there. That made him cocky. He got so brave and comfortable that he would wave his arms, stick his tongue out, and holler when they approached.

Immune from consequence, he took to singing songs he'd heard from his father anytime they came near. "Whack for my daddio, whack for my daddio, there's whiskey in a jar!" Nothing he did gave him up.

Leprechauns. He was sure of it.

The pot-o-gold at the end of this rainbow ended up being the moonshine he was making. He'd constructed a crude still by cobbling together a stolen cook-

ing pot, his condenser, and a clay bowl. He cooked better mash and had real sugar and yeast. Later, he found a barrel to use as a thumper. But the real magic of his 'shine came from "secret ingredients."

As a lark, he mixed things into the brew that he found in the cave. Little clay jars of multicolored powders were arrayed on a shelf, hidden in the corner of the room where he slept. Sitting among the jars in this "apothecary" was an Indian corn doll with short, black hair and little leather breeches. Each container had a different stick figure pattern drawn in its clay top. He could make out representations of fish, salamanders, crawfish, and turtles. When he opened the jars, they each had a unique aroma. Some were so interesting he tasted them. Even more interesting. He experimented adding the powders to his brew.

The first batch he distilled blew his mind. Almost immediately after drinking, he saw light from the sunset refracting obliquely as the world around him lost focus. Waves of bubbles washed across his field of view. Floating in place, he swayed back and forth gently, a cold, wet feeling rushing past his cheeks and down his sides.

Another week, another flavor sample mixed into the brew, he had a different mind-altering experience. In this iteration, he felt himself sink into a gooey coolness as soon as the alcohol hit, again with a wavy, out-of-focus feel to the surroundings. Darkness enclosed his head as he withdrew from the light, quickly sinking into a pleasant unconsciousness.

With every jar he took a different journey into another world, another reality. Awakening from the experiences, he felt more a part of the nature, specifically the creatures of Appalachia's waters. He became addicted to these novel sensory travels, replacing his past life of privation with new journeys into unknown environments. He no longer cared to live a not-drunk life. That life was desperately lonely, sobering up to hunger in a cold cave watching it rain outside.

"Robert!" hollered the sheriff. "Robert Lazar Bubb! We know you're here. Somewhere around here anyway. You need to come out and give yourself up. You gotta leave. You don't have a choice. Not that anybody cares, but it's not safe to stay here. Not no more. Come on, boy! Gotta go!"

"Come on out you sorry stealin' sneak," yelled the man from Georgia Railroad and Power, the owner of the land where the moonshiner was squatting, the

man's voice nasal and high-pitched.

"Come on outta dere, or eben yo' dreams'll be wet!" shouted a deputy, winking at a buddy who doubled over laughing at the joke.

Robert was a thorn in the side of Tallulah's Law enforcement. They could never seem to catch up to him. Neither could security officers from the railroad and power company, who'd lost food and supplies from their dam project down the river. It would be a relief to all of them when this pilfering parasite was in jail.

"Robert, we both knows you cain't swim," one of the men cackled, the rest laughing at the moonshiner's expense. "Last time you fell drunk into Warren's pond, we had fun watchin' you drown."

Another deputy howled; "You was blue when we yanked you out. Coughed for a month, as I recall. Pitiful," he said, shaking his head, pausing for effect. "But hilarious!"

"Hey, Sam. I got an idea," said another man. "We should let him stay put. Set up chairs on the high ground, bring along friends and watch the show!" They doubled over laughing again.

The deputy giggled uncontrollably. "Robert's a hoot thrashin' around, tryin' to keep his head above water. That face he makes when he gives up hope and sinks is somethin' ya' gotta see."

Robert heard them making fun. He had no intention of giving himself up. It was true that since being at the grotto he'd never, ever tripped and fell so much. He'd tumbled so hard, falling on rocks painfully. Even drunk he'd never had so many accidents. But he knew he had it good. He was going to stay right where he was. Despite slipping sideways into the creek more times than he could count, feeling like he'd been pushed, he was staying. Or having big evergreen branches slap him in the face when walking down a path. This was as good a life as he'd ever had. Even when his face got pushed down into his food by who knows who, it was a small price to pay to be in this magical place.

At any rate, he knew they couldn't touch him. He wasn't afraid. For the first time in his life he felt safe. And nobody was going to lay their damned hands on his kick-ass moonshine. Nobody. "It's all mine," he kept repeating to himself. "I ain't sharin'."

To celebrate his circumstances, the advantage that he had over the lawmen, he decided to try mixing up a couple of the powders. He'd make a "Super Hooch" with the moonshine he had left. Grabbing a couple of clay jars randomly, he stumbled over to his jug. He curled up a magnolia leaf and channeled a touch of the three new ingredients into the concoction already inside.

Poof. A rainbow mixture of powders shot out of the jug. The cloud of colors spun into a dust devil, glittery flints of light rising between the canopy of the trees. The jar of moonshine shook in his hands, a swirling foam spilling out the top. "This oughta be good!" Robert exclaimed as his hair blew back, raising the liquor to his lips. He gulped it down, wide-eyed with anticipation. "This gonna be the trip of a lifetime, fo' sure."

CHAPTER TWELVE

Robert woke up shivering, cold, and very wet, as miserable as he had ever been. Headache, nausea, a weird feeling in his neck, …, no hangover ever felt this bad. Eyes burning, shivering, ears feeling plugged, both of them needing to pop, …, he wondered if he'd taken too many of the powders together. He'd remember next time not to do that, he hoped.

Being by nature oblivious, he hadn't been very observant about the goings on downstream on the Tallulah River. Isolated as he was, appropriating the 'little people's' rock grotto up Eden's creek, he was unaware there were plans to create a lake deep enough to rise above where he slept. As the lawmen joked the day before, the soon to be named Lake Rabun was actively filling in the ravines between the mountains.

He'd been stealing food and supplies from workers at the dam construction site. But he didn't think to connect the construction of the dam to the actual consequences of a dam. After all, who in their right mind would stop the wild, booming flow of the river that defined the area and attracted so many tourists? It was beyond Robert's comprehension.

*J*ack realized what was happening as he watched the young moonshiner and the series of events unfold. He knew the history of his lake. What Robert didn't know, what he would never know, was why they built Mathis Dam. It was 1915, and the Georgia Railroad and Power Company needed hydroelectric energy to supply the new streetcars in Atlanta. There would be seven total dams down the length of the Tallulah, with the river's awesome power quieted to supply electricity for a growing "New South." The character of the area would radically change from the thunderous roar of the Tallulah River to picturesque mountain lakes. Once the series of dams were complete, the river's past glory would be lost. The stream through Tallulah Gorge was an impotent reminder, the flow held to a mere trickle by comparison to days past.

Robert's latest moonshine binge had him out of commission, sleeping for what seemed like days. It was a hammer to the head, little enjoyable about it. It left him feeling ruined, his vision blurred and the light around him diffused in a deep green/brown shimmer. Most disquieting was a sense that he was floating, unable to get a good foothold on the ground.

Looking up, the sun's light spread out in ripples, as if he were underwater.

It was then Robert realized, first with confusion, then shock, that he was underwater. He frantically tried pushing off the bottom to get to the surface. But he slipped on the muddy lakebed when he tried. Not for the first time, he lamented never having learned how to swim. It was too late to learn now.

Thinking this was it, his last moments alive, he got mad. He thought of the sheriff and the deputies calling him out. Making fun of him. But letting him drown? That was going way too far. Letting him die, just for moonshining and a little petty theft, …, well, that was pretty low. A low thing to do, especially for a church-goin' lawman. Standing there and letting a man die who was just trying to get by. Pretty low.

In his self-pity, though, Robert realized that he wasn't, in fact, drowned. He was just floating in place, perfectly buoyant, well below the surface. He wasn't gasping for air or choking, either. Other than everything looking dark and blurry and feeling pruned-skin wet, wet to the bone, he seemed fine without air to breathe.

Understanding that nothing he did changed his circumstance, Robert tried to reason out what was going on. "I'm dead," he thought. "I'm not struggling to breathe because I'm already a goner. That's got to be it. And this is what happens when you die. It had to be those crazy powders I put in my hooch," he reasoned. *"Too good to be true, that stuff was, and it did me in. I overdid it, and this is what it's like on the other side."*

But he didn't see flames and his skin wasn't roasting. So this wasn't Hell. Miraculously, he thought, he had dodged the devil. On the other hand, there were no pearly gates or roads of gold. He laughed. Everyone knew that wasn't going to happen. Looking up at the glistening surface of the new lake 20 feet above, he had no answers, only questions.

Jack watched as the Yundwi Tsunsdi *gathered by the shoreline of the still rising waters. Alongside them was the Cherokee dark demon* Ka'lanu Ah-kyeli'ski, *a Raven Mocker, impatiently waiting for the moonshiner to surface. It had been lurking by the water's edge, promised by the 'little people' that it could have the moonshiner first. It was scanning the lake, thinking that its victim would pop up soon, hoping there would be some hint of life. The* Raven Mocker *relished the thought of eating his favorite delicacy, the still-beating heart of a dying man. It knew that by consuming the organ it would restore youthful vigor into its aging flesh.*

Near him towered the fur-covered Tsul 'Kalu, *a fire-eyed* Sasquatch. *He'd worked his way down through the forest from his mountain ridge cave to take advantage of the flood and its consequences. He'd been aware of the bothersome human, the thorn in the side of the 'little people'. He'd been amused about the distress the man caused, smiling at how the* Yundwi Tsunsdi *had so much trouble shooing him away.* Tsul 'Kalu *would let the* Raven Mocker *get the heart, but he wanted first dibs on the moonshiner's surely flavorful liver.*

The Yundwi Tsunsdi *begged the fabled creatures for assistance well before the flood, asking for help to rid them of the human pest. Neither the* Sasquatch *or the* Raven Macher *chose to provide assistance. But today they both showed up, thinking they'd have easy pickings. Floods killed indiscriminately, even planned ones, and this one promised hearts and livers to spare.*

Losing their home to a flood inspired the Yundwi Tsunsdi *to again consider moving up their migration. All were anxious to reconnect and recharge with the Great Spirit,* Unetlanvhi, *deep in the earth. Having their home flooded prompted calls to move the timeline for departure to now, the young moonshiner no longer a concern.*

Yet something about not seeing the body of their squatter felt wrong to the 'little people'. Incomplete. Suspicious. Peculiar. Confused by the no-show of their dimwitted antagonist and unsettled about their impatient and hungry mercenaries, the Yundwi Tsunsdi *wanted the wet corpse of the moonshiner retrieved. They felt a strange, difficult-to-explain need to tie up loose ends. They asked the* Nunne'hi *"Water Tribe" to swim down and investigate.*

After a few minutes, the divers returned, stupefied. The human was alive, but not in a way they could have expected. The squatter in the "Rock Tribe's" grotto wasn't struggling for breath when they found him. Unable to swim, he was flailing around in the submerged cave. And while he seemed completely alien to his environment, he wasn't suffering from being underwater, either.

The consensus of the members of the "Water Tribe" witnessing the spectacle was clear. The young moonshiner had undergone a supernatural transformation from an air-breather to an underwater breather, strong magic at work.

Upon hearing this, the giant Tsul 'Kalu *tromped off to look for other victims of the flooding, other drowned mammals with fresh livers sure to be found on the shore. It was going to be a day of death for many of the Great Spirit's creatures, a day of feasting for the* Sasquatch.

The Raven Mocker, Ka'lanu Ahkyeli'ski, *was not so easily redirected, so consumed by thoughts of the young man it could already taste his bloody, pulsing heart. It dove into the water hoping its victim was within reach. But it got dark within a few feet, forest refuse from the muddy, rising waters shielding him from seeing. Even with supernatural abilities it couldn't locate its prey. Frustrated, it decided to search for dying humans elsewhere.*

———————————

Days later, after unsteady and frustrating progress scaling the rocks of the underwater grotto and over to the shoreline of the new lake, Robert was able to climb his way out. The crowd of "little people" had dispersed long before. He pulled himself up and lunged onto the bank. Rolling over on his back, he rejoiced at the feel of the sun on his skin. But his mouth opened and closed, repeating an automatic, rhythmic O-shape. He couldn't breathe. The gills, …, did he really have gills? …on his neck opened and closed, pathetically incapable of function out of water. Heartsick, Robert rolled back into the lake. He could breathe again.

Slowly, by necessity, Robert learned how to work his way through the water. Over time he accepted the fact that he was incapable of leaving his new environment. It was a sick joke, the young man thought, given his lifelong fear of drowning. His world was upside down, inside out. And, for one of the first times in recent memory, he had no means to either find or consume liquor to escape his woes. Of course, liquor never filled his biggest hole, a lifelong overwhelming loneliness, with no prospect for a friend in sight.

As months went by, the Yundwi Tsunsdi *gradually put the pieces of 'Moonshine Bob's' unexplained survival together. Much to their embarrassment, they realized their culpability in the human's transformation. Their first mistake had been their relationship with Joe Cherokee, giving in to their innate fascination with twin children, something that all the supernaturals shared. The boys being so young and with no obvious signs of bad intent were allowed too much freedom in their camp. When the boys begged for help from the 'little people', sharing elementary magic with the two seemed an innocent thing. Giving a few breadcrumbs of mystic knowledge to the youngsters didn't seem to be too far outside of the Great Spirit's design. At least it didn't at the time.*

When one twin brother tragically drowned, the 'little people's' empathy for the remaining survivor led to even more forbidden magic let loose. Never expecting the Indian child could succeed in magically concocting a potion to protect people from drowning — the boy himself having abandoned the attempt — they didn't fear the moonshiner using the boy's old array of magic-infused powders. Not being mindful of the consequences of giving magic to a child inadvertently enabled this bothersome pest of a human to transform.

But it was done, and the question became "What to do now?" The Yundwi Tsunsdi *had to begin their migration. But they couldn't leave this inhuman alive. This mistake-of-empathy would throw off the natural balance they were meant to uphold. It forced them to confront the truth that they had not one, but two creations causing the disequilibrium. Both were their fault and without fixing both mistakes they would further delay their plans. The Indian boy, now grown to be a man, was the other muddled mess that needed resolution.*

Jack woke up to a head full of stories. It felt like he'd shared a mind-meld with the 'little people', Joe Cherokee, and 'Moonshine Bob'. He learned the two men were intrinsically linked to each other and the forbidden magic of the *Yundwi Tsunsdi*. They were disruptions in the natural order, misused supernatural power, and they needed to be dealt with by the gods that allowed their creation.

Questions accompanied Jack to the breakfast table. How had 'Moonshine Bob' managed to stay alive all these years? He'd been a plague on the lake for over a century. Had the *Yundwi Tsunsdi* tried and failed to rid the lake of their problem? Did 'Bob' turn out more powerful and magical than they were prepared to face? Or had they not "handled" him because they didn't want to also get rid of Joe Cherokee, with whom they had a special relationship? Did they attempt to enlist other supernaturals in the effort?

And the story stopped short of explaining 'Moonshine Bob's' relationship with the lake monster 'Herman'. Jack had to be satisfied with the explanation given by Joe Cherokee during his "initiation."

More personally upsetting to Jack was how the *Yundwi Tsunsdi* knew Joe Cherokee's life had to end at their hands yet acted like everything was fine. Weirdly, Jack even had empathy for the moonshiner, who he realized was just a naïve experimental chemist who made Joe Cherokee's potions work by accident, combining it with his homebrewed liquor. Was it the young man's fault he ended up a lake troll? Yet Jack knew the moonshiner had "gone to the dark side," his heart turning when he awakened and began using 'Herman'. It was a decision to choose evil.

It troubled Jack. Did every possible scenario have the 'little people' ending Mr. Joe's life and killing 'Moonshine Bob' to restore balance? Couldn't they just be stripped of their powers and banished to live out their lives in peace? Maybe on a Pacific beach in Mexico. Live in grass huts. Bob could learn to distill tequila while Joe creates a better sunscreen for his new apothecary. You know, build a brand new order out of the chaos of revoked citizenship.

Easing off the outdoor couch, Jack got up and opened the doors to the kitchen. The 'little people' were everywhere, but there was no more noise from clanking pots or slamming cabinet doors. Clumsy attempts to remain concealed weren't necessary. They just looked up at Jack and smiled. One even started whistling.

"Good morning, Mr. Joe," Jack said. "And good morning to you, too, Pop."

"Morning,' Pop replied. "Did the *Yundwi Tsunsdi* 's "Dreamworks" production of the origin of 'Moonshine Bob' answer enough of your questions?"

"I learned how he magically ended up an obligate water-breather. And I'm not happy how 'Moonshine Bob', the *Yundwi Tsunsdi,* and Joe Cherokee all are supposed to end up," Jack answered. "Can anybody explain why it's taken over a hundred years to figure out how to get this resolved?"

"*Ah,*" Mr. Joe exhaled. "*The heart of the matter.*"

"The elephant in the room," Pop echoed.

"*The core conundrum,*" Mr. Joe rejoined, "*continuously unconfronted.*"

"We could continue to cowardly collate the causes for why we can't seem to confront this concern," Pop smirked, looking mischievously at Joe Cherokee. "And animated alliteration is an admittedly aggravating and annoying way of avoiding answering arguments from anyone who asks."

"You guys don't seem very torn up about the 'little people's' plans to remove Mr. Joe from their "to-do-list,'" Jack broke in.

"That's because it's not so much Joe's problem as it is the *Yundwi Tsunsdi's*," Pop answered. "The Great Spirit, *Unetlanvhi*, has challenged them. If the keepers of balance don't learn from their mistakes, this problem could resurface. The 'little people' are a proud bunch, not used to being taken advantage of by children or mistakes of omission with drunken, hapless humans. Joe Cherokee and 'Moonshine Bob' have been living on borrowed time, awaiting the lesson from the Great Spirit to be understood."

Mr. Joe broke in; *"I'm not holding them back. I'm at peace moving on. The next phase of my existence, the one where I leave this particular reality, is a mystery, sure. But I understand and look forward to restoring the natural equilibrium. I embrace my humanity, the one where I was born of a woman, live, and die. When young, you may wish you could live forever. Yet there is a beauty in the cycle of life. Cheating death is cheating the truth of our place in the Great Spirit's world."*

"Until the lesson for the 'little people' takes, we wait," Mr. Joe revealed. *"The supernaturals must answer to the highest power, too."*

"Meanwhile," Pop interjected. "I get to have more time with the most interesting friend a mortal man could ever have.

And Herman wasn't recognized as being so dangerous until recently," Joe Cherokee added. *"That kinda snuck up on us."*

Across from the cove, on the hillside opposite Jack, a family awakened to fear. The oldest son, a divorced man in his 50s, didn't join the family at breakfast. He was last seen by his sister putting up their boat. He brought her home after attending a "Rabun Book Club" social at a lake neighbor's home the evening before. He told her to head up to the cabin and he'd take care of things on his own.

The family hadn't expected him to be there when they woke up. He'd planned to go out early to fish with a friend. But a nephew spotted the man's glasses in a cup holder above the dash of the boat. He, too, had fishing on his mind and walked down to drop a hook in the lake. He'd found their boat loosely pulling against a bow rope on one cleat. Wakes from early morning skiers rocked it back and forth, floating high and light in the water.

Calls to the man's fishing buddy went unanswered, an agreement between the men to "unplug" when out together unfortunately misfiring. The family's concerns grew.

'Moonshine Bob' would have told them not to bother trying to call. He was gone. Time to move on.

After telling his sister to go upstairs, the man sat down and relaxed on the front edge of the deck, admiring the evening sky. His face showed a gentle smile and half-closed eyes. He laughed and threw a small stone out into the lake. Shaking his head, he laughed again, obviously entertained by the events of the day.

'Moonshine Bob' hated the way the man looked. A grown man surrounded by family, happy and content. A day just finished that made the man smile and laugh. 'Moonshine' never had a day like that. It made him sick. He wondered what put the man in such spirits. Probably a woman. Those were feelings he'd never had, either. The whole picture of the man on the deck made him resentful. Angry. And he knew what happened when he got angry. His "pet" would come up from the depths, keep him company, and do his bidding.

As if on cue, a broad wave made its way towards the scene, ominous in the evening light. 'Moonshine Bob' sensed his ally's presence as the big fish moved in by his side. He held the monster back, knowing there'd come a point in time where he'd know to enter the fray. Something out of the ordinary always seemed to present itself. Leave an opening. Bad things happened to good people, even without villains like him helping. He preferred to lend a hand, of course, but a tragic accident was something he could wrap his head around, too.

The man stood up on the deck and went to secure the boat, wondering if he should park it inside, pull it up with the lift, and unscrew the drain, or leave it here to use in the morning. Maybe he should leave the boat and drive his car to his friend's house instead. Whatever he did, he had to get his glasses out of the cupholder. He leaned out and put his foot on the port side gunwale.

That's when he realized he hadn't secured the stern. Obviously distract-ed, he chided himself as his legs did a wide split over the water. As far as boats go, he'd always been intentional, practiced, and mindful of things that could go wrong. That's why he was quick to volunteer to pick up his sister. He was the responsible one.

Not this time. His mind was elsewhere, on his girlfriend. And he was going to get wet. Big deal. Worse things could happen. A dunking could be fun, something silly to tell his sweetheart. A new family story. He smiled and held his nose.

His splash was awkward, a three-quarter belly-flop, with his left shoul-der rotating down, deep and fast. That's when things went from a mo-ment of physical comedy to nightmare fuel. Spinning towards the dock, the man's neck got snagged by a big, silver lure with a menacing triple hook. It was his nephew's overlarge choice out of his uncle's deep-sea tackle box stored in the dock's locked closet. The boy thought it was the perfect tackle to catch the submarine-sized striped bass he'd seen swim-ming under the lifted boat inside the dock several times this summer.

The young man cast the monster lure a couple days before. Casting was hard in the limited space, and his control of the rod showed it. He whipped it too fast across the boat slip and moaned as it wrapped around a support post. Quickly pulling back, he hoped it would free up. But the tackle slipped a few feet further down underwater and the boy popped the line. He got called upstairs and forgot about it.

Flash forward, and now two hooks were deep into the man's left carotid artery, each one cutting and tearing as he writhed in pain. Not knowing what to do as the line was taut and he'd expelled his remaining air, he tried kicking himself off the underwater supports of the dock. But his foot slipped through crisscrossed support beams and got stuck. Real-izing the trouble he was in, his eyes bulged open in terror, his mouth gaped wide as blood rose in clouds from his neck.

"That's a face I can relate to," 'Moonshine Bob' thought before the man's eyes closed and his head bent over. "And we didn't have to do a durn thing." 'Bob' looked over to his monster, thinking about the unfairness of life and how it caught up with this unsuspecting, cheerful person.

Upset he wasn't the one to hook the man's neck, he consoled himself that he got to see such a stupid accident take a good man's life. But, even if he'd taken part in what killed him, that wouldn't have put out the fury he felt, the anger at his situation.

With the man dead along with the dissolution of the moonshiner's evil thoughts, the *Nun'Yunu'Wi* slowly sunk back into the dark depths.

CHAPTER THIRTEEN

Grandfather came down to the dock as Jack finished his after work, afternoon swim. He looked down at Jack still panting, trying to catch his breath at the ladder. Jack could see the old man wore his swimsuit under his white cotton robe. He knew he should stay where he was. Pop liked to tread water and talk.

Most people treading water would sink when they talked, having to stop, breathe in to regain height above water level, and then restart their conversation. With no vest, you need a chest full of air to float. With air escaping with each spoken word, it was … glub, glub, glub if you tried a long sentence.

Not grandfather. Talking and floating? No problem. He could float for hours, taking advantage of his overly large chest. This extra bouyancy was an advantage. Jack inherited Pop's lungs, working like giant air bladders to help him float higher and with less resistance. This was an advantage in competitive swimming. Add in his grandfather's long arms and hyperextending knees, each adding an extra few inches of power to his stroke and pull and to his kick, and you knew why Jack excelled in swimming early on.

Pop dove off the deck and did a couple of butterfly strokes before flipping, diving well below the surface, and rising next to his grandson. Jack's heart ached when he saw his grandfather work out arthritic stiffness and worn-out joints in the morning, wincing and moaning at the effort. But the old guy was still agile and powerful in the water. Using both hands to get water out of his eyes and wipe back his thinning hair, Pop started talking.

"You deserve a better explanation as to why 'Moonshine Bob' is still around," grandfather began. "Proverbs 3:11-12, do not take the Lord's discipline lightly or lose heart when you are reproved by Him, for the Lord disciplines the ones he loves."

"Yeah," Jack replied. "You left it scribbled on a notepad on the breakfast table this morning."

"The 'little people' are supernatural beings, not used to having to reflect on mistakes. Taking human lives because of a mistake they made is not in their nature," grandfather continued. "The Great Spirit, *Unetlanvhi*, requires they learn to uphold their prime directive regarding the balance of nature, including any consequences of their actions."

"It's been hard for me being in constant contact with supernatural beings that are outside my faith," grandfather explained. "My personality seeks explanations. Logical, rational explanations. I thought I'd been able to separate my faith from reason. And then the *Yundwi Tsunsdi* dropped into my life."

"I think of the 'little people' like our idea of angels, but there are major differences. *Unetlanvhi* is awaiting a sort of repentance from his *Yundwi Tsunsdi* for the problems of Mr. Joe and the moonshiner. Christian angels don't have a human soul. They can't be forgiven. And there's no equivalent in the Bible for angels needing to migrate deep into the earth to refresh."

"Still, there is no doubt we are surrounded by supernatural beings well known to the Cherokee," Pop said. "The Indians and their gods interact, with no need to rely on faith to believe that they exist. You and I also know they exist. In a way, we're living out "materialism vs faith," one of the conflicts at the heart of ontology. The reason I could "let go and let God," allowing you to come into our circle, is because of my belief. My faith doesn't need material confirmation. Same with the wiser-than-you-might-think Joe Cherokee. We're ready to balance the scales. But the 'little people' aren't similarly equipped. That's why it's taking time."

While grandfather and Jack were treading water and sharing "Deep Thoughts," the *Yundwi Tsunsdi* were busy upholding their side of the bargain. Finally. Perhaps they were inspired by their young recruit and the new energy he brought to the old men that shared the cove. Because they were failing in the eyes of *Unetlanvhi* and weren't comfortable how to proceed, the elders of the 'Rock Tribe' made a choice. They decided to follow a suggestion made by Joe Cherokee. The Indian thought they should consult the powerful god *Ocasta*, who'd enlightened him in his own quest to understand his situation.

Mr. Joe thought it was about time they listened.

The 'little people' knew of *Ocasta*. His place in the hierarchy of Cherokee gods was loftier than the *Yundwi Tsundi*. The Great Spirit used *Ocasta* to stir things up. By reputation difficult to predict, the god would champion chaos one day, allow for order the next. Better things were frequently born from destruction of the norm, the chaos of change forcing creative thinking. Advancement of cultures was harder when everyone was comfortable, seeing no need for change.

Ocasta was not a favorite of men. Frustratingly close to finishing a project, people would turn around and find that product of hard work and planning was lying in shambles. His unpredictability made him disagreeable to be around, even for the supernaturals.

But things had changed for the god, explained Mr. Joe to the 'little people'. There was a reason to reconsider taking his counsel. *Ocasta* was not only easier to approach these days, he'd been transformed into more of a positive reflection of the Great Spirit, *Unetlanvhi*.

Unknown to the *Yundwi Tsunsdi*, the change in *Ocasta* was because of man. Years before - much to the god's surprise and never-ending embarrassment - a woman, using only her wits and a sharp stick, had trapped him. Her tribe managed to throw Ocasta into a fire in hopes of killing him. They'd grown tired of the god destroying their works, were unhappy with the chaos he caused, and felt it worth the risk. Frustrated that they couldn't build a more comfortable life, extreme measures were needed.

Being a god, *Ocasta* wasn't killed by flames. While he was burning, instead of being killed, the best of his nature miraculously coalesced. Fire made him transform. In his new, enlightened state of being, he did something different. He chose to reward the ingenuity of his human captors, granting them glimpses into the blessings of knowledge, wisdom, and power. Many of those Indians became accomplished Medicine Men.

Hearing that *Ocasta* had a conflict with humans and changed gave the 'little people' hope, and they sought out his advice.

The 'little people' presented their problem to *Ocasta,* outlining their responsibility for Joe Cherokee and the moonshiner. They understood what they should do to restore balance. They explained their hesitance in putting Mr. Joe to death. But, from what Joe Cherokee told them, Ocasta himself had given humans new powers. Why wasn't he being held to account. Why were the *Yundwi Tsunsdi* being punished for doing the same thing as the great *Ocasta*?

Ocasta laughed. "The men who captured me were defending themselves from my destructive side. The side of my nature that emerged from the fire was forgiving. Acknowledging their bravery and craftiness in capturing me, I chose to share a glimpse of the magic available to them in the natural world. Teaching them which mushrooms gave visions and what herbs could provide contentment to a troubled soul was a reward to people who were only trying to preserve what I repeatedly destroyed. I did not give them anything that would disrupt the equilibrium between man and nature.

"Your tribe of *Yundwi Tsunsdi*, on the other hand," Ocasta continued, "made naïve choices that disturbed nature's balance. While you may have reasons for assisting the child, the world we gods inhabit doesn't care about justice or injustice. Perhaps seeing such sadness caused by the brother's death, observing how devastating it was to the survivor, led you to inappropriately share forbidden skills. But, over time, this ended up creating the "evil" moonshiner who couldn't drown, emerging in response to the "good" child who had supernatural skills. Neither belongs in the natural world."

"*Unetlahnvi* created me to expose the world's inhabitants to extremes of form and chaos, your tribes to manage balance between the natural world and man. When choices contrary to your directive occur, the Great Spirit seeks to restore that balance by teaching you 'little people' a lesson. You have no choice. You must make plans to dispatch both creations, no excuses."

CHAPTER FOURTEEN

The Lake Rabun community always looked forward to Independence Day. The morning began with the July 4th Road Race, the fastest runners usually from the local high school cross-country teams. The narrow lanes of Lake Rabun Road shut down to through traffic the early hours of the holiday for the run. Any and everyone is encouraged to participate. Elderly "speed walkers" share the road with pregnant mothers pushing strollers, all following the ridiculously curving course from the Lake Rabun Pavilion to the end of the big basin and back.

Jack liked to run the race with his mother, an SEC track athlete in her day. But both of his parents were at the beachfront on Florida's highway 30A with 'Grams' this Fourth of July. He was a little jealous because later that evening the beachgoers would see fireworks displays all along the shore from Rosemary Beach through Alys Beach and beyond. The white sands of the "Redneck Riviera" were packed with sunworshippers from affluent suburbs all through the Southeast.

Not wanting to race alone, Jack corralled a few guys from the Y-camp and dressed their "team" in Cowboy hats, American flags, and Kazoos to add to the fun. They played John Philip Souza's military marches they'd practiced the day before. After running a mile, they stopped and played "Stars and Stripes Forever." After another mile it was "Semper Fidelis." In front of Pop's house overlooking the road they accompanied Pop and his porch speakers to "The Washington Post."

Highlighting midday was the Classic Wooden Boat Parade, with the highly polished mahogany restorations all in a line sporting patriotic flags, red-white-and blue bunting, and skippers with Uncle Sam top hats. The wealthy on Lake Rabun saw ownership as a prestige thing, and the single-file line of cruising wooden boats was a chance to show off. Favorites among the boats were assorted Chris Crafts – Rivieras, Racing roundabouts, Special Roundabouts, a 17' Deluxe, and a Sportsman – along with a couple Garwood Commodores. All were from the heyday of these pleasure craft, most of them constructed in the late 1940s and early 1950s.

Lake Rabun's Boat docks had an undeclared competition, with the more ostentatious having not only flags and bunting, but music and LED light displays. July 4th being the most attended lake holiday, seemingly every dock was crowded with onlookers waving flags. They were all trying to get the attention of the parade's trailing antique fireboat, hoping to get sprayed by its powerful firehose. The bright noon sun made a rainbow out of the stream of water making an arch between the prized firefighter and second-story observation decks.

No matter how much they waved and screamed, Pop, Mr. Joe, and Jack couldn't get the parade close enough to entice a shower from the boat. Jack used to think their cove was too much of a detour from their route. Now older, he realized they just didn't have a row of shapely coeds hanging off the upper railings to attract the firefighters. As if to make his point, a dock across the lake was enjoying a fresh shower sporting just such a scene. Jack hoped that next year, as an upperclassman, he might get a few of girls on the team to come up for the experience. Of course, that would only work if he could talk Pop and Grams into going to the beach. That would guarantee a wardrobe upgrade sure to gain attention.

Everybody's favorite part of Independence Day was the "Fireworks on the Fourth," a large display shot off the earthen dam on the western end of the lake. People drove their array of crafts close, everything from pontoons to ski boats idling in the bay to watch and cheer. Hotel-sized mansions would be packed with observers a few hundred yards from old lake cabins with white-haired ladies. Y-campers could appreciate the fireworks from the camp's hillside, so Jack was a free agent.

Joe Cherokee asked if Jack could take him along tonight, saying he was a fan of the noise and smoke of the show, something Jack knew was out of character for the Indian. Mr. Joe gave Jack another curious excuse for joining Pop and him, claiming he wanted to celebrate the day with the loudest and the brightest celebration the lake had to offer.

Getting there early, Pop and Mr. Joe made themselves comfortable on the rear bench seat of their decades old ProStar 190. They counted on Jack to keep them away from other idled, drifting boats, grabbing a long oar and positioning himself on the front of the hull. He passed the time until the crowd showed up playing patriotic country music on the boat's antiquated sound system. The three joined others in the vicinity singing a chorus of "And I'm proud to be an American, where at least I know I'm free, and I won't forget the men who died and who gave that right to me ..."

The fireworks show didn't disappoint. Boom, Boom, Boom, ..., the deafening sound of the choreographed explosions was a perfect end to Rabun's day of tribute to the good old USA. The display had all the various tried and true categories of fancy mortar shells. Several "Palm" with their multiple sparkling tendrils exploded above, followed by "Comet Stars" and crisscrossing "Crossettes." But the biggest and the loudest were the "Peony" and the "Chrysanthemum," giant round patterns bursting color shot off together in groups. Other mortars exploded with glittering silver rain, whistling sounds after the initial bang, and scintillating shimmers of gold, the latter in showy "Willow" displays.

The finale was a cacophony of large, different colored mortars going off every five to ten seconds accompanied by a long row of fused Roman Candles arrayed on the dam shooting sparks and smoke into the sky. It concluded with scores of reporting concussive rounds echoing off the surrounding mountains. When finally over, the subsequent quiet was broken by loud "whoops" and clapping from the boats and docks full of family and friends who'd enjoyed the show.

After the cheers and applause died down, the basin began to empty. Boaters floating nearer the dam, like Jack, were still engulfed in sulphureous smoke and were in no hurry to leave. Those in the rear of the Inner Basin, parked there for this specific reason, lined up under the watchful eye of law enforcement from the Department of Natural Resources to beat the crowds heading home.

Returning by boat from the fireworks display was always risky, especially given the near-total darkness of a new moon night. Red and green lights on the stern and bow of the boats were for identification, not to illuminate the waters ahead. It was hard to navigate as the meandering shoreline and a few known landmarks were often in total darkness, difficult to see. Like everyone else, Jack struggled to stay safe, big boats with big wakes all around. Veterans of the ride back to their home docks stayed single-file and slow. But visitors to the lake, unaware of the potential risk from unseen, extreme waves, opened their throttles soon after getting far enough away from the DNR.

Turning into the Big Basin with the Narrows in sight at the distant far side, an aged ski boat timidly accelerated. It was dangerously overloaded with the waterline close enough for the kids on board to dip their hands in the lake. The anxious driver captaining the craft was struggling to avoid turbulent water, his boat handling poorly from the weight. His head on a swivel, he made every effort to steer clear of danger.

Unfortunately, captains of newer, larger, and safer craft were getting brave. With the crowds thinning out and the promise of home ahead, they were oblivious to the overcrowded accident-waiting-to-happen. Two Bayliners rapidly approached the smaller boat's stern on either side, engines brought to a roar as they accelerated past. Water poured over both sides, swamping the boat and its screaming teenaged occupants.

Jack came out of Pigeon Mountain Run several minutes later and saw the commotion caused by the foundering boat. He saw they were positioned where the lake opened into the Big Basin. He'd arrived just as the endangered craft seemed to stabilize, almost all nearby boats having stopped to minimize waves. There weren't enough life jackets for the number of passengers. Teens who were better swimmers had already bailed out, hoping to lighten the weight and keep the boat from sinking into the black-as-night water.

Then Jack saw something from the corner of his eye. An ill-defined, broad wave of water was rising, heading their way. It came from Eden Creek cove aiming straight for the nearly capsized craft and its terrified teens.

"'Herman'," Jack said to Pop and Joe Cherokee, pointing towards the swell.

"'Moonshine Bob' must be in a mischievous mood," Pop replied.

"And those kids are in trouble," said Mr. Joe.

The cresting wave shaped by the giant fish struck the starboard side of the boat with great force, capsizing it. Those sitting on the gunwale were thrown out in varying parabolas of flight. The vessel flipped over and began to sink.

Slowly approaching the accident, Jack idled the engine. Taking off his shirt and shoes, he channeled his inner lifeguard and jumped in. With Joe Cherokee shining a high lumen, waterproof flashlight underwater, Jack dove down and looked to see if anyone was trapped below the boat. Pop threw life vests out to the wide-eyed youths flailing about in the water. Officers from the Department of Water Safety finally arrived on the scene and took over, happy that civilians hadn't died trying to be heroes.

All seemed safe with no casualties. Jack thought that fate gave the youths a pass. He hoped the accident scared a few of them into not doing something so stupid again. The men knew the kids would have to face whoever owned the borrowed boat and be punished. And a ticket would have to be paid for too many passengers on board. But the secret the three of them shared was knowing who capsized the boat. The accident drove home the fact that 'Moonshine Bob' and 'Herman' were accelerating the frequency of their actions. With each attack, the monster grew and the challenge the two presented seemed more insurmountable.

CHAPTER FIFTEEN

Jack woke up congested and coughing. Wayward summer colds and GI bugs ran through Y-camps like grass through a goose. He remembered the chunky, red-headed kid coughing in his face days before. At the time, he was so focused on monsters below the sailboat that he didn't dwell on it. And now he had a cold. Blowing his nose into a Kleenex, he announced his illness to the men before he headed down the stairs to the kitchen.

"Whoa there, boy," Pop cautioned. "Stay where you are and give me a minute. I knew when you told me you'd be here this summer that this day would come. Viruses plague youth camps everywhere and I knew you planned to be a counselor. So I got prepared. I researched the issue and the result is in that drawer." He walked over and pulled out a wide, clear plastic bottle with a small black nozzle. "I mixed up a nasal rinse specifically for this possibility."

"Your nose wash have any of my "medicinals?" Joe Cherokee questioned. *"I'm missing some of my stash."* Besides a thriving business in mushrooms for friends with "anxiety," Mr. Joe had a side hustle of herbal hallucino-

gens. Local healers used his "stash" to ease the pain and worries in the remaining months of life for their hospice patients.

"I've got a few things in my cupboard to help fight off colds," Mr. Joe went on. *"Herbal mucolytics, cough suppressants, and immunity boosters are all there if you need them, Jack. They're better fresh. Some of those herbs might do well used with Pop's nose wash, too."*

"I didn't have to raid your herbs, Joe," Pop explained. "It's just a simple recipe with water, salt, baking soda, and a touch of povidone-iodine. Squirting it up both sides of the nose is supposed to protect you from viruses and bacteria. I was researching an Asian Indian medical journal and ran across it. It was part of the reason that year's worldwide viral pandemic wasn't as lethal to communities that used it as a preventative."

"The authors said the mixture helped India do well, even without expensive vaccines and biologic medications. The rinse softened the spread of the illness, a much more logical plan than shutdowns. Hiding from everyone just puts off catching the virus. And India has a lot of high-risk patients. Since a much lower percentage of them died, I thought it would be worth trying."

"Jack, you know I'm not against Cherokee medicines," Pop said, not discounting Mr. Joe's source of income. "In fact, from what I've seen, mushrooms are underutilized and undermarketed. With so much stress and tension out there, Mr. Joe should probably start talking to health food stores about wider distribution. I think he ought to start advertising to women with anxiety, displaying them next to bath salts. Label them "Psilly Joe's Psillycybin." I'll give him that brand name free of charge."

"Did you know that Mr. Joe was once invited to lecture at Ole Miss?" Pop asked Jack. "It was for the groundbreaking of the natural products division of the Department of Biomolecular Science. Their School of Pharmacognosy had heard of him, no doubt because they study indigenous people's herbal remedies for active, therapeutic properties. Centuries of experiments, trial and error from ancient healers, shouldn't go for naught. And, if a viable drug is discovered, it can be very lucrative."

"Because of our friendship and my interest in biochemistry, I almost chose that career path," Pop revealed. "There's something empowering in finding healing substances occurring in nature. Cherokee mythology explains that for every illness there's a natural cure. How cool would that be to prove as true? A way of acknowledging the Great Spirit's works and being thankful."

"By the way, Joe, I'll let you use my steam shower as your "sweat lodge" substitute anytime," Pop said as an aside. "But don't abuse the privilege. That funky odor, …, musty, almost rotten, I haven't been able to get rid of it," he complained. "Whatever you used in there, please, don't do it again."

"Uh, …, I didn't used anything in there," Joe Cherokee chuckled. *"No mushrooms. No nothing."*

Jack laughed and water came out his nose.

Pop, looking at the two, joined in laughing, but his was more nervous than joyful. He wondered if he should ask the odor's origin. Deciding that he didn't want to know, he closed the medicine drawer and went to the sink. He bent over and irrigated both sides of his nasal passages with his virus preventative. He sprayed the sink clean and blew his nose in a paper towel. Ta-da. But he felt drainage and coughed again.

"Good thing your Grams isn't here," Pop laugh-choked when he straightened up, spewing a fine, orange-red mist over the just-washed dishes, making him need to clean them all over again.

After the laughter settled down, Jack turned to Mr. Joe. "I've got a big day ahead on me," he whined, "They can't spare me at camp. Everyone's out sick. You said you might have something for my cold?" To add emphasis his request, he coughed and sniffled, slumped his shoulders, and gave the Indian a pitiful, pleading look from his reddened eyes.

"*Sure,*" Joe Cherokee replied. "*I told you I have medicines that can help.*" Joe reverted to his spaghetti-western, fake Indian voice. "*Whether helps or not, you pay heap big wampum. Me not on your insurance plan. Out of network.*"

Serious again, Mr. Joe began to list pharmaceutical items to compound. "*Let's see now, …, rose hips and honey, of course. Add some dried mullein leaves for congestion. Sumac for the sore throat. You do have a sore throat, correct?*" Jack shook his head yes. "*Golden seal boosts the immune system and skunk cabbage thins the phlegm. I'd add some willow bark for the inflammation, but your OTC aspirin option is stronger and easier to dose.*"

"All that?" Jack marveled. "Sounds like a lot of work to collect and store."

"*Golden seal, for sure,*" Joe Cherokee replied. "*It's an art to find, gather, and put up native healing plants. Your grandfather and I have been collecting them for years. Just like fruit, there's a window of time when they are "ripe and sweet" before they quickly decompose. Herbs must be gathered at their peak. Then they are dried in the sun, but only after the morning dew has evaporated away. Digging up medicinal tubers is also time-specific, most potent when collected as the plant is about to flower.*"

"I help when plants are scarce or time is pressing," Pop interjected. "Bad weather can make for a last-minute change in plans. A week of rain can mildew and mold, ruining a harvest. It can also rush the picking, doing it before they've "ripened." That's the major problem the wineries in this soggy county share, making the differences in year of harvest so noticeable."

"I'm willing to try anything to get better, Mr. Joe," Jack said, sniffling for emphasis.

Joe Cherokee acknowledged his request and turned for the back door. After going to his creekside cabin, he returned with an array of lidded Mason jars. Jack took the items Mr. Joe directed and then hopped in his truck, too late to go to work by bicycle.

Once at the Y-camp, he already seemed to breathe easier, his cough also calmed. Through the morning it was apparent he'd been rescued by his grandfather's Indian friend.

After a sunny morning of outdoor activities with most of the boys playing horseshoes, clouds began to move in. They had a classic camp lunch of baked beans and a hot dog cooked with a stick over open flames. Keeping the glowing coals going, they made S'mores, stacking graham crackers with chocolate and a campfire-roasted marshmallow in between. Just as the treats were finished, an early afternoon rain shower forced them inside.

The campers chanted, wanting a dance lesson. They'd seen a favorite female camp counselor clogging at a dance event the week before. They wanted to learn the local "hillbilly dancing" mainly because of the girl, but also because they liked the dance's rhythm and energy.

Jack borrowed the girl from the nearby camp. They pulled up recorded banjo and fiddle music from the eating hall sound system and the girl stomped and clapped in demonstration. The boys crowded around mimicking her moves. After an hour, some of them faked it well enough to get by.

When the rain stopped, frogs croaked in grateful harmony. The sun dappled freshly through the light-green leaves of the poplars and needles of the pines. The hot and sweaty initiate cloggers shed their shoes and shirts and sprinted down to the lake to cool off. They may never become serious "hillbilly" cloggers, but the boys got what they wanted, another chance to see their pretty camp counselor dance.

Jack returned to an empty lake house, recovering well enough from his cold to do his training swim. He went upstairs and changed into a clean Speedo swimsuit, an old one with his high school colors. He put on his cotton robe drying on a hook and headed downstairs to the kitchen.

Herbs left on the counter caught Jack's attention. Joe Cherokee's natural remedies were helping so far. "Must be my next dose," he thought to himself. "Thanks, Mr. Joe." There was a note underneath the handful of seeds and leaves that read "chew thoroughly." Jack brushed the mix off the counter and into his cupped hand. He followed instructions, chewing thoroughly, probably more than required.

He finished and wound his way down the steps and across the road, then down the stone and cement steps to the boathouse. He surveyed the course ahead, looking all the way across the basin, hung up his robe, and walked out to the deck "starting block." Assuming a racing stance, he checked the time. Then he sprung from the boards, race-diving to begin the swim.

The first three-hundred yards he maintained a good rhythm. The water was calm as most boaters were in for dinner. He wasn't coughing and all seemed well. If seen from above, there'd be nothing to suggest a problem. It looked like a routine, uneventful exercise. But that didn't last. Jack started to drift, first towards the shore, then away. His strokes lengthened and then he just dolphin-kicked, arms forward. Then he dove, broke through the surface and dove again, strong kicks and streamlined shoulders and head behind his outstretched arms. Not travelling fast enough to maintain his orca-like swim, each breech was less high and graceful. Then he dove vertically down, submerged quite a while before returning to the surface, his path degenerating into a splashing, spinning, flailing ordeal.

Shaking his head and looking around, he turned and headed back to the dock. While he still struggled to swim a straight line, zig-zagging and frequently stopping to look around, he made it back to the sandy shore at the rock wall behind the boathouse. He sat on the wooden

steps down from the deck to the "beach" and waited for his head to clear.
Then he climbed the remaining steps up to the second story deck and
onto the futon bed, covering himself with a couple robes before falling
asleep.

CHAPTER SIXTEEN

Jack awakened from his nap hearing the footsteps and conversation of Pop and Joe Cherokee. He still felt a little off after what he guessed was a crazy reaction to the Indian's cold medications. The two men crossed the bridge to the covered second deck and Jack on his futon. They'd just gotten home after an all day scavenge for herbs and mushrooms for Joe Cherokee's "cupboard." After a fresh summer rain, finding happy, peak-potency plants was how they had fun.

Mud-caked and soaking wet, they walked through the sliding barn door entry to the second dock. Their soggy clothes stretched from water weight hung off their shoulders and hips. Their sleeves hung past their hands and they were walking on their pants. The brims of their hats fell over their ears. Jack thought they looked like waterlogged sheepdogs fresh from a mud bath.

Jumping into the lake was a welcomed ritual after a successful forage.

Depending on the number of people nearby, they would either strip and leap off the platform naked or jump in fully clothed. Lots of neighbors today, so they walked off the edge feet first, holding on to their hats and pinching their noses. It was eleven feet down to the water's surface and another 13 feet to the sand and aquatic plants on the lake floor. Mr. Joe had biodegradable soap in his pocket.

Jack was anxious to talk but let them clean up first. They brushed the mud off their clothes, unbuttoned and unzipped under the cover of water, and tossed the rinsed items onto the deck. After working soap into their hair, under their arms, and around their privates, they submerged to rinse.

Fresh robes, courtesy of Jack, were waiting for them near the steps where the men climbed out. It was something the not-so-bashful old men frequently "forgot." Robed, they gathered their heavy, wet clothes, walked up to the bridge, wrung out the shirts, socks, and pants, and draped them over the rails. Pulling out chairs and sitting down, they were finally available to engage with Jack. The clean smell of eucalyptus and mint came in with the men.

Before they began talking, Joe Cherokee looked at Jack and tilted his head, squinted his eyes. "You look strange, Jack," he said. The Indian took a moment to scan his face, read his posture and the rate of his breathing. He recognized something from Jack's unfocused gaze and dilated pupils. "Did you take those herbs off the counter?" he inquired as if he was putting a puzzle together. "If you did, I'm glad you're back on land. That medicine was meant for an old, dying woman who's in severe pain and suffering great sorrow. One of my hospice doctor friends was supposed to pick it up today. That was a two-week supply. Not wise to take that stuff and do anything but lie down and "escape.""

"So, I took hallucinogens?" Jack asked, already knowing the answer.

"At that dose, and with everything else in the mix, …, absolutely," Mr. Joe replied.

Jack looked at Joe Cherokee, letting the reality of what just happened in the lake sink in. He rewound the sequence of events from his swim and was getting new insights each time he reflected. The men could almost hear the gears in Jack's brain working as they watched. They chose not to interrupt. Like Pop always said, "Don't bring an umbrella to a brainstorm." They waited, leaning forward, fascinated, not saying a thing. After a couple of minutes staring into space, Jack looked up.

"Gather up the clan," Jack said firmly, grim determination in his voice. "Everybody needs to hear this. It's about 'Moonshine Bob' and 'Herman'."

The *Yundwi Tsunsdi* joined them, curious, not used to being summoned. Neither Pop nor Joe Cherokee had ever proposed action against 'Moonshine Bob' or 'Herman', especially with the lake monster grown so intimidating and powerful. Now, this young human demands their presence. Intriguing, but sure to come to nothing, the supernaturals suspected. Yet perhaps the Great Spirit *Unetlahnvi* was behind this venture. The 'little people's' inaction in redeeming themselves had been an embarrassment to them. And *Ocasta* had given them a hard ultimatum. They had to do something soon.

Once gathered, Jack began to talk. Joe Cherokee acted to help with communication, in case colloquialisms and issues with modern English got in the way. "Something very interesting happened this afternoon during my training," he began. "It involved the monster in the lake. I think, from what I've learned from this afternoon's interaction with the creature, that a new way forward can be considered. It's something that might allow for success in battle with not only the fish, but 'Moonshine Bob'."

Jack hoped that by taking agency it wouldn't offend the 'little people'. Up until now, he thought it wasn't his place to assume he could. Then again, up until now he hadn't wanted to do anything this summer but have fun and save some money. Live the life. He thought he'd be satisfied and content having all these outdoor adventure options, always occupied, sometimes even excited, never missing out.

Well, life made different plans, Jack realized. At first, it was Pop trying to educate him, give him an understanding about decisions and their consequences, and turn him into a grown-up. Then, of all the potentially crazy things that could ever happen, it turns out there are supernatural beings living all around him. And they're involved in a dangerous conflict with enemies he couldn't get anyone to believe were real. It isn't a situation anyone could pretend away.

Jack knew it was time to leave the unserious behind. Time to let go of the sense that responsibility is a bad thing, something others could do for you, something that could be put off. Time to grab a chance at fulfilling your destiny, not doubting that's what you're doing. This might be what you've been groomed to do your whole life. Time to embrace it.

Jack was worried about the plan he was about to propose. It had holes, flaws, and assumptions. But he knew that good leaders don't always have perfect answers or perfect plans. What they had was the ability to visualize victory and get others to believe, enter the conflict with an attitude that made the other side doubt themselves.

"I may have discovered a means to occupy the Shoggoth and leave 'Moonshine Bob' vulnerable," Jack said matter-of-factly. "This is the advantage we might all have been waiting for."

Pop, Joe Cherokee, and the *Yundwi Tsunsdi* were justifiably curious. A grin broke out on Jack's face. He wanted the clans on board, and having their attention was the first step. While it was obvious they had no idea what a Shoggoth was, all their white-haired heads tilted forward, drawn in to hear what would be next.

"While training, I made an unexpected connection with 'Herman', the lake monster," Jack began. "As I swam, the huge creature was cruising the deep waters beneath me. As usual, the 'Water Tribe' was shielding me from harm. But this time something unusual happened. It's something I discovered that shines a light on a vulnerability. Something that can disrupt the static back-and-forth. Something that could give us advantage, finally make peace in our cove, in our lake. It's something I discovered by mistake."

"Walking into the kitchen after camp, I found herbs on the counter left by Joe Cherokee," Jack told them. "I'd been sick and was already a lot better using his medicines that morning. I believe it was a poultice and other decoctions. I thought he'd left me additional treatment to use when I got home from camp. Happy with my recovery so far, and not wanting to miss the opportunity for further improvement, I chewed the mixture of seeds, dried flowers, berries, and mushrooms. Then I went down to the lake to train."

"Joe told me after the fact that the mixture wasn't meant for me. The stack of morning glory seeds, mushrooms, and red saber I mistakenly threw into my mouth were for a dying old woman being cared for by one of Joe Cherokee's friends. When given in small doses spread out over time, Mr. Joe said, they can unlock treasured memories or provide a pleasant fantasy for the sick to inhabit in their final days. As it turned out, I took two weeks' worth of the herbs all at once."

"After essentially overdosing, it gave me crazy hallucinations," Jack continued. "And swimming with such an altered state of mind was terrifying. But it was also fascinating and magical. My swim started out with no issues. At the middle of the Big Basin the drugs began to kick in. I imagined the lake's crows – with their "caw, caw, …, caw" frighteningly loud – divebombing me from their high perches in the pines on the shore. I plunged underwater to escape. Needing to breathe, I breached the water imagining myself as a killer whale. But I wasn't, because when I looked to the sides I had wings. A rainbow formed from the mist falling from my feathers. I dove again and found myself inside a massive, luminescent bubble, a magical work-around for my need for air. Going deeper, I pushed the air-pocket until I came face-to-face with 'Herman," its undulating body reflecting my light as I approached. It was understandably startled to see me at that depth. We looked in each other's eyes."

"After a moment of disorientation, I had to close my eyes," Jack continued. "Then I shook my head to clear it, opened my eyes, and was looking at my image glowing inside a bubble. I was looking at myself looking at the monster, watched and being watched simultaneously."

"I wondered, was I seeing myself through 'Herman's eyes? Were we sharing the sight? Obviously, we were. Mr. Joe's herbs managed to allow me to infiltrate and then occupy the mind of the Shoggoth. There can be no other conclusion." Jack looked around, wondering if they understood the implications.

"Just as I realized my altered consciousness had gotten into 'Herman's' brain, the creature realized the same thing. It didn't like it, shaking its head, bucking like a bull shaking off a rodeo rider. Nothing changed. The monster closed its eyes and re-opened, like turning off your computer and turning it on again, hoping it will reprogram. It didn't matter. Furious, it charged at the bubble enclosing my body."

"Shaking my own head "to reboot," I tried to pull out, get back to "reality." I struggled to separate from 'Herman' and protect myself from its threat. As the beast rushed towards me, my consciousness-shared body in a pocket of air, it missed, like a bull tricked by a matador. I think the 'Water Tribe' must have pulled me out of harm's way. Soon after I was on the surface, again thinking the underwater clan's efforts brought me up more than my own. It was just me treading water, not an orca, with no feathers, and not surrounded by a bubble. But I was still tripping."

"I lowered my head back underwater and searched for 'Herman'," Jack continued. "I imagined the creature looking up at me, confused, unsettled. I knew the incident stunned it, because we shared more than our vision. We shared each other's reactions. I felt fear in the beast. It felt my fear, as well."

"Still frightened and high, it was like I forgot how to swim. I wasn't sure where my unglued brain would lead me next. Remembering the monster was after me, I made my way towards the boat dock. On the way I was surrounded by craziness. I witnessed the strange sight of my arms stretching out wildly like the rubber-armed Reed Richards of the Fantastic Four. Then I dodged stones dropped from above by massive eagles, birds big enough to carry a wizard back from Mordor. As I came close to shore, Mermen bared their shark-like layers of teeth, ready to bite."

"Somehow, I manage to get to the beach and climb the wooden steps out of the lake," Jack recalled. "I went up the stairs and crashed on the futon bed. Pop and Joe Cherokee woke me up when they came down to swim. After they cleaned up, we talked."

"I learned of my overdose. Sitting there, wet, dizzy, and scared, I pulled a wild idea out of my mind-expanded, hypercreative brain. Without the herbs giving me out-of-the-box thinking, I'd have never thought I could use my new skill; monster-mind-melding consciousness."

"My proposal is this," Jack began, hoping the group could fill in the particulars as he went along. "We agree that 'Moonshine Bob' has escaped fate because of the ally he has in the Shoggoth. For years the lake monster has been psychically linked to the moonshiner, growing with each evil action. Like Shoggoths in literature, he receives dark thoughts broadcast by the depraved and villainous, awakening from unconsciousness for the chance to fulfill any dark deed their inspiration desires." 'Moonshine Bob' has been its only guide for a very long time. But Shoggoths like 'Herman' are not relegated to merely one master."

"My idea is to interrupt the connection between the monster and the moonshiner, rerouting 'Herman's' focus. I've occupied the monsters mind already, so I know it can be done. We know which of Mr. Joe's medications facilitate the link between us. Neither 'Herman' nor 'Moonshine Bob' has known anything but each other's immediate availability. If contact isn't right there for them, I can see them being confused, especially the moonshiner. This first step of the plan must work. Unless we disconnect them, I think they're too strong for us."

Jack stopped to let his last thought settle in with his audience. All eyes were glued on him. Nobody was walking away laughing. He knew that was a positive thing.

"Once I invade 'Herman's' consciousness," Jack continued, "I don't think I can hold him long. He'll want to break free from me sharing his brain. He'll attack me if he can find me. The next task will be a more personal challenge. Summoning evil to activate the monster and capture its mind. This isn't in my nature. Having dark enough thoughts to bond with the Shoggoth may be a bridge too far. This may be where I could use help from the *Yundwi Tsunsdi's* supernatural allies, the ones I saw waiting to eat 'Moonshine Bob's' liver and heart when they first filled Lake Rabun."

"*Tsul 'Kalu*, your fire-eyed *Sasquatch*, has a special power. He hypnotizes anyone who sees him, bringing people out of "Oh my gosh, is that Bigfoot?" into "What? Did I see something? Nah." It's the way he's managed to remain a silly fiction rather than a monstrous fact." Hearing nobody disagreeing, Jack went on. "I'm sure he still wants the moonshiner's organs."

"With me and 'Herman' in a battle for brain control, I'll be near the shore. The monster will be near the surface. I want the Sasquatch there, hoping he can use his powers to deceive the beast's mind. Anything to obstruct the communication to 'Moonshine Bob', so the rest of you can arrange for the *Raven Macher* to take him out."

This is where Jack's formal ideas ran out. He couldn't imagine the 'little people' putting anyone to death. But he knew the *Raven Macher, Ka'la-nu*, was quite capable of the task, as his desire for the moonshiner's still beating heart was well known. In Cherokee stories, the Raven Macher was the last thing seen in this life before moving on to the next.

Several minutes of quiet followed Jack's presentation. Jack worried whether his plan was well received, whether they considered it realistic. The timing of his experience could be a sign of assistance from a higher power. If anyone would be receptive to this possibility, Jack thought it would be the group around him now.

"I have to tell y'all," he finally said, breaking the silence, "that after distracting and confusing 'Herman', the rest of the plan is yours. Enrolling *Tsul 'Kalu* and *Ka'lanu* are just suggestions. I pulled them in having learned their roles from your Cherokee stories. And I know that something, some higher power seems to be guiding us through my visions. Again, if you think this is a true sign, we should follow it."

CHAPTER SEVENTEEN

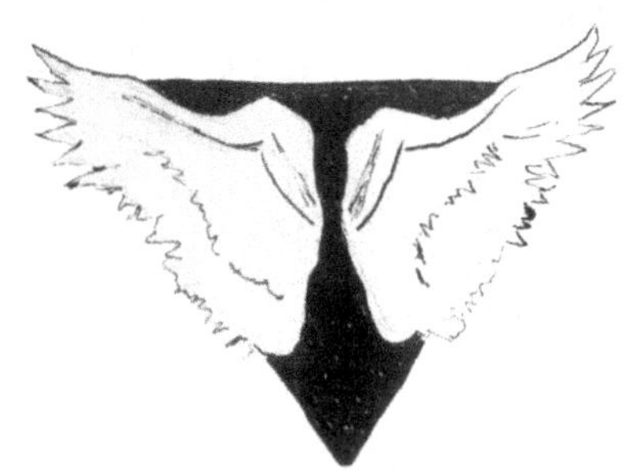

Joe Cherokee listened patiently to Jack's long speech, feeling a combination of fascination and fear. The young man was suggesting they trust him and follow his lead in a very dangerous plan. Jack came up with his idea after a few minutes of hallucinatory imaginings after overdosing, thinking he was strong enough to distract a monster by occupying its mind. It made Mr. Joe very concerned he would lose Jack, destroy his friend Pop, and not be around to help him recover.

But at least the young man had an idea. Given no plan had ever been proposed, the Indian felt they had little choice but to try and move forward. He knew he'd have important responsibilities in any plan they formulated, doing things that had never been tried before. Yet, he chose to trust the possibility of success. Despite the unknowns, something felt right.

While Joe Cherokee admired Jack stepping up so soon after being recruited, he also felt guilt he'd done essentially nothing to move things along. He should have acted long ago. But, in his defense, part of his inaction revolved around knowing the 'little people' getting rid of 'Moonshine Bob' involved getting rid of him as well.

The 'little people' shared the blame, of course. The bond between the supernaturals and the now-grown surviving twin was strong. They knew Joe Cherokee's time was supposed to be limited, but taking his life wasn't something they were accustomed to doing. Until lately, 'Moonshine Bob's' actions hadn't been so awful, either. But his recent endeavors made him hard to hide from *Unetlanvhi*.

The ancient Indian enjoyed his extended life on the Great Spirit's beautiful, green earth. For a very long time he had concerns about what was next. But clinging to an artificially long life he knew to be selfish. It felt increasingly wrong. Eventually his time with Pop led to a revelation. The bond he felt helped him realize his lack of trust in a higher power was behind the fear. Identifying the problem let him finally find the way past it.

Joe Cherokee saw the missing tiles in Jack's mosaic of a plan and knew he could improve on it. He also knew his fate was the piece into which most others fit. He decided to take initiative, with the help from the *Yundwi Tsunsdi,* and create his own plan forward. It had to be him initiating the event, as *Unetlanvhi's* lesson was clear.

Jack's grandfather pulled him aside after his presentation. He complained that he couldn't see a way to be useful. With Jack's life possibly on the line, how could he stand by helpless and incapable of assisting his grandson? He wondered if Jack might not understand the risk he was taking. While he was proud that Jack knew what he was fighting for and Pop respected his bravery, was he aware of the gravity of the situation?

And relying on the 'little people' and their supernatural cohorts was akin to herding cats. From his time spent with them, Pop didn't think they'd "play well with others." They weren't natural teammates. "All for one and one for all" was not in their lexicon. They didn't view death and dying like we do. Pop felt it was time to get back to "Deep Thoughts."

"As you're aware, Jack, the 'little people' are nature's stewards," Pop began. "While the natural world functions better working in equilibrium, it is not an arbiter of morality. In nature, the strong dominate the weak. They eat them, kill them, enslave them, and use them for their pleasure and amusement. The choice you're making to fight evil suits the 'little people's' need to restore the balance they desire, but they may not care whether you survive the effort."

"Joe Cherokee lived his early life around these earth-bound supernatural entities," Pop explained. "He didn't need to accept their existence by faith. He knew them. Before you and I encountered them, being Christian believers, we had accepted the supernatural exists here on earth on faith alone. Meeting and interacting with unexpected supernatural beings is an entirely different animal for us. As Christians we might assume these entities work within a similar moral code to our own. They don't."

"The *Yundwi Tsunsdi* seem to behave in a moral manner to me, Pop," replied Jack, focused for a change on grandfather's ontologic ramblings. "Unless that's me projecting."

"You probably are, Jack," Pop agreed. "Our God is above and wholly separate from nature. He made humanity self-conscious, a difference from other natural creatures. As a result, our hearts grieve for the innocents. We have compassion for the downtrodden, defend truth, and seek beauty. We believe that our hearts reflect God, a God we know to be one of love."

"Joe's *Yundwi Tsunsdi* are material beings that don't practice Judeo-Christian ethics. Through Joe's interaction with believers, he's educated himself regarding the Christian God. In his heart he already knew intuitively that He exists. Accepting God's goodness is a leap of faith, and Mr. Joe has made that leap. He read that God heard the suffering of the Hebrew under tyranny and used Moses to lead the Exodus. That's the difference of our God. Through the Bible, Mr. Joe came to know there is a foundational morality outside of the natural world. The *Yundwi Tsunsdi* have different priorities in relation to man, despite their apparent deference for the twin child that grew up to be Joe Cherokee."

"That's what I mean," Jack said. "Their tenderness for the child implies caring." Jack hoped his grandfather would see the 'little people' the way he did.

Pop smiled at his grandson, happy he wasn't daydreaming through his "Deep Thoughts" like usual. "Ultimately, the Indians and their gods are of this earth," Pop continued. "Our God is outside this earth. Yet His essence pervades everything. God is present even in the outsider and the foreigner. As such, the Cherokee supernaturals don't stand in conflict with our vision of the world. They can co-exist with our faith. Mr. Joe came to understand this, recognizing His underlying Truth while not abandoning what he knew to be real in the *Yundwi Tsunsdi* and the other gods of the Cherokee. Don't judge my friend when he talks of the Great Spirit, as *Unetlanvhi* is the face that provides Joe Cherokee comfort."

"God called us to fight evil, Jack. His supernatural message is distinctly different than the natural processes of this world. It is a theology that calls for moral purpose. Mr. Joe knew he had within him a desire to do good. He understood that by doing good he confirms and reinforces the existence of a higher power outside of nature. Doing good supports our Higher Power's intent."

"I'm telling you this for several reasons. Our Indian friend is comfortable with his fate. You don't need to worry about him when the time comes for him to go. He has found his peace. You, on the other hand, would be risking much more. You could die well before your time. Before you can impart my wisdom to your own grandchildren. That frightens me."

"But I have faith that you will be in God's hands. Unlike your old grandfather who thought he could protect everyone and handle things himself, I'm letting go and letting God. But I'd like to know you're going into this conflict with your eyes open, only counting on yourself, Mr. Joe and me, hoping you recognize how God helps as well. Don't count on the 'little people' to magically save you, whether you live means little to them."

"But they could save me, ... right?" Jack pleaded. He'd grown to like them and think of them as friends.

Pops shoulders lifted and he gently shook his head. He really didn't know. It was another instance of not knowing despite gathering every fact he could, something that used to drive him crazy. Crazier. He'd spent decades trying to reconcile Cherokee supernaturals, not knowing what he didn't know until the unbelievable happened. His belief that all things could be explained if you studied them hard enough was being mocked daily. At least he'd learned to "let go." That's what he kept telling himself.

He looked at his grandson and smiled. "Mr. Joe and I will do all that we can. I'm trusting that you are a survivor and will live. I know Joe Cherokee will not. He's finally doing what men are supposed to do. He'll pass from this world. It's how it should be. Life as we know it is worth more if there is a beginning and an end. The Lake as I know it, without my enemy, will be entirely different, too. Don't forget the 'little people' will try and catch up on the migration after all is done."

"What will you do?" Jack asked, since Joe Cherokee, 'Moonshine Bob', and the *Yundwi Tsunsdi* occupied a large part of his day.

"I've never been good at community," Pop answered. "That needs to change. Maybe I'll help teach medicine. I've done a little of that and enjoyed it, even though I'm "rural" medicine now. I could volunteer more at Foxfire, the Appalachian Cultural Museum, sharing what Joe taught me about gathering and putting up herbs and mushrooms. Primitive life in the Southern mountains was unforgiving and the Cherokee helped the settlers when they could. The Clayton Rotary is dedicated to truth and service and is doing good works. I'll probably attend church, too. That's something your grandmother likes a lot, and a happy wife …"

"Is a happy life," Jack said, nodding his head up and down, grinning. "You could try "slam poetry," Pop, making up lyrics as you swim, striking the water for the rhythm. Or update the songs in your head."

"Of course, there's you and the rest of the family," grandfather continued. "I'll be redefining my role. I'd like to be remembered as more than a curmudgeon."

"Too late," Jack smiled. "Try all you want, but you can't pretend to be anything else, even without your lake monsters."

CHAPTER EIGHTEEN

The *Yundwi Tsunsdi* had been on the porch since before dawn. Rabun being Rabun, it had rained through the night and showed no signs of stopping. Days like this upheld the county's claim to be the wettest east of the Mississippi. Clouds were low, the mountains surrounding the lake nowhere to be seen. You couldn't prove they existed. Indifferent to the rain, the 'little people' were anxious for the day to begin, the day everything changes. The day they make things right with the Great Spirit.

Unlike the rest of the players in this drama, the environment was always the same for the moonshiner. The only change was the daily cycle of the sun and the moon, the phases of the latter each month leaving him in intolerable darkness. Lake Rabun's clear water would shimmer ribbons of gold in the midday sunlight, transparent well into the depths. But today was just another heavy grey sky. Another day filled with routine and boredom. Another of the many days accompanied by the sound of rain on the lake's surface, a soft tinkling he'd heard far too often, like bits of glass bouncing off a metal screen.

Joe Cherokee solemnly hiked the hill from the creek cloaked in his waterproof poncho. Underneath the raingear, he'd chosen to wear his old buckskin breeches and a beaded, striped shirt, a tribute to his youth and his tribe. It hung in his sleeping quarters reminding him every morning that he was Cherokee. He'd added a neck wrap of different colored bandanas loosely tied. Arriving at the porch, he joined the 'little people', leaving his poncho on. He didn't want the theater of his homage spoiled; his last act made predictable.

His past few days had been spent in their company, making plans in a sacred cave within Minnehaha Falls. They had done all the talking required. Now was the time to be quiet, visualize the game ahead, think of how to be prepared for the unexpected. Despite Joe Cherokee's knowledge that this was his last day, at least in his current "manifestation," his face radiated peace.

Jack woke up after a fitful night's sleep. He knew he was taking a real chance today, and the gamble was nearly all his, as his grandfather said. Jack hoped "battle plans" were made concrete between Joe Cherokee and the *Yundwi Tsunsdi*. When last they talked, things were too "off-the-cuff" for his liking. "Slipshod" would be another word for it. A miracle-if-it-really-happens-that-way story he hoped would pan out in his favor. But he had faith. If the faith slipped even a little bit, he'd think of his allies and feel stronger. Through them his faith was "unreasonable."

Parts of today's plan intentionally kept Jack in the dark, at his request. He didn't care to know how Joe Cherokee would be "taken care of." A strange euphemism, he thought, wondering how the phrase originated. He didn't care to witness the killing of 'Moonshine Bob'. He worried that on Judgement Day he'd be visited by the two, each killed by his plan; murders done indirectly, but murders, nonetheless.

To keep himself focused on his role, Jack repeated the words of 'Hillel the Elder'. "If not me, who? If not now, when?" Pop's "Deep Thoughts" useful, again.

Jack wasn't sure of his grandfather's role in the plan. But he had faith the old guy would protect him. Why stop now, after so many decades "on duty"? Pop and Mr. Joe had spent hours together after the *Yundwi Tsunsdi* were through with their "rehearsals." They mostly shared gratefulness in having met. Jack saw them forcing smiles, trying to maintain composure. Their show of manliness was betrayed by the tears running down their cheeks.

"Well," Jack said to no one in particular. "Great things don't happen by themselves." He spun and got out of bed. "Like Napoleon said – if he spoke English, anyway – audacity is always the right approach. Unless it's more audacity than is required."

Pop wasn't sure how he felt about the day ahead. He feared for his grandson. Despite years of interaction with the 'little people', he didn't trust they would make protecting Jack a priority. In the grand scheme of things, a man's death meant little to them. He and Joe Cherokee made plans accordingly. Towards that end they made a pact. Their nemesis would be gone and Jack would be free by the end of the day.

Grandfather ached imagining a life without Joe Cherokee. He loved him like his brother. But he was happy for Joe at the same time, proud his friend was at peace, rising above the need to be brave witnessing his upcoming last, unselfish act. Mr. Joe told Pop to fill the void of his absence not only with memories, but future acts, tributes to what they believed in. He assured Pop he'd be with him in spirit when the time came.

Joe Cherokee stood with Jack inside the boathouse, out of the rain. There was quiet determination hanging in the air between them, like the conductor of an orchestra looking at the first violin, ready to start the Symphony if front of a packed house. Mr. Joe's herbal hallucinogens were in a Cherokee Indian ceremonial bowl between them.

Jack was to chew just enough of Mr. Joe's concoction to make initial contact with the lake monster, 'Herman'. The Indian didn't want to dose it as high as Jack's last experience, where he was terrified and out of control. He needed his wits about him. Joe Cherokee would stay with Jack until the mind-meld was complete, the connection made when Jack was seeing out of the eyes as the Shoggoth. Then Mr. Joe would give Jack a "booster" dose to last long enough to complete their plan. After chewing the herbs, Jack would jump in the lake to see if the monster reacted as he had before. Shielded by the iron-like locust wood dock posts and close enough to the sandy beach and wooden steps for an escape, Jack would try and lure the predictably angry and charging 'Herman' close to shore where the *Tsul 'Kalu* stood waiting.

Jack rehearsed the scene in his head, the last act a vision of the monster fish in a mind-control battle with a Bigfoot. He couldn't wait. Imagining himself on the top wooden stair, he'd have a front row seat to a battle too crazy for anyone to believe. The flame-red eyes of *Tsul 'Kalu* glowing while he attempts to hypnotize the *Nun'Yunu'Wi*, the fish struggling not to let it, all so 'Moonshine Bob' would be left alone, outnumbered, doomed to be confronted by the Raven Macher. If he could get the 'little people' to sign over the movie rights, he'd be set for life.

Here, Jack's fantasy stopped, not wanting to be haunted by the expression on the doomed subaquatic hillbilly's face when he's charged by the Shoggoth, the fish's massive tail flicking him up on shore, the Sasquatch's evil intent overriding the moonshiner's control of its brain. He would have to look away when 'Moonshine Bob' saw his heart, still beating, removed from his chest by the Raven Mocher as he dies. Gruesome. That part of the movie he'd have to miss, make an excuse to go for popcorn and a drink.

Giving Mr. Joe a hug, the game began.

Joe Cherokee splashed a new, different powder into the herbs and mushroom mixture Jack recognized from his previous "bad trip." He passed the ceremonial bowl to Jack, advising him to take the smaller amount he'd parceled to the side. It looked to be a quarter of the amount he'd taken before. Jack took the measured amount and put it in his mouth, "chewing thoroughly" as instructed. Then he closed his eyes and focused on 'Herman'.

While Jack tried to recreate the pharmaceutically induced connection with the consciousness of the monster, his grandfather was doing his own connecting. The 'Water Tribe' was working to get 'Moonshine Bob' away from the dock, using Pop as the bait. Given the creature's decades of frustration with the old guy, the guardians of the cove felt it wouldn't be hard to accomplish. He'd been number one on the moonshiner's "to-do list" since he was a teen and managed to escape his grasp.

Never actually threatened in their long conflict, 'Moonshine Bob' had grown complacent. Comfortable. He didn't need to question whether he was safe. But, today it was his turn to be first on Pop's "to-do-list."

Once the 'Water Tribe' located "Moonshine Bob," they relayed the underwater site to Pop. Adorned in his rain poncho, he stepped arthritically into his Mad River Canoe, cast off from shore, and went out to fish directly over his intended prey. Casting a few times, he made a show of it, using live shad as bait to catch the striped bass that had been stocked into Lake Rabun decades before to attract sport fisherman. He acted out what he'd seen unsuccessful fisherman do; cursing the lake and its bad reputation, cursing his luck, cursing the fish for not biting, and cursing the wet weather as a puddle formed in the canoe, soaking his shoes and socks.

Intentionally casting into a fallen tree, the tips of its remaining branches barely submerged, Pop's lure hooked and irretrievably imbedded itself, just as he planned. Yanking and flailing, Pop stood up in the boat while tugging, the line managing to get more tangled with each pull. Rhythmically timing the tugs just so, he caused the unsteady canoe to rock back and forth, back and forth, until it tipped over, spilling him into the water.

'Moonshine Bob', who'd been doing all he could to keep fish from biting Pop's bait, couldn't believe his luck. Pop treading water, alone with no supernatural protectors in sight, was not normal. It was a chance he couldn't pass up. He bolted up from the depths to grab his nemesis and pull him under. The moonshiner flashed back to the last time he had him dead to rights, decades before.

But he stopped halfway up, sensing something was wrong with 'Herman'. There was an unfamiliar void when he tried to connect with the Shoggoth. Attempting to invite his "pet" over to get into the act, their mutual enemy so vulnerable, he came up short. He focused his evil thoughts harder. Still nothing. He sunk into the darkness as he tried to understand, no longer caring about his prey.

The moonshiner knew something was fishy, no pun intended. His lifelong enemy was all-too-easily there for the taking. He just happened to flip into the water right on top of him. And it happened at the same moment he couldn't call 'Herman', the one thing in his entire life he could count on. It was awfully suspicious. What were they up to? His breathing got faster as his head turned to sweep the water around him. What had they done to interrupt his connection with his monster?

He decided to see for himself. Changing his focus from Pop to 'Herman', 'Moonshine Bob' started swimming towards his ally, getting angrier as he approached the last place he'd seen the beast.

Pop, meanwhile, had been scanning the deep water with his swim goggles in place, using any means to see the moonshiner's advance. It didn't take long. Only seconds after bailing out of the canoe he saw the raggedy fish-man, his remaining white hair and long beard flattening past his ears and shoulders as he rose from the deep. Just as he hoped. Just as the water tribe of the *Nunne'hi* laying in wait around him planned.

Then Pop saw him stop. "No, no, no," he screamed into the water, bubbles erupting around his head. 'Moonshine Bob' began to sink and turn around. "No!" Pop exclaimed again, screaming, terror in his voice.

Leaving the poncho to drop, Pop abandoned the swamped boat and swam to shore. Clambering up the hillside, he got to the lake road and took off, fast-hobbling on his bad knee around the horseshoe bridge and up the hill towards the stairs back down to the family boat dock.

'Moonshine Bob' was almost across the cove, bearing in on Jack, menace in his rheumy eyes.

At the same time, 'Herman' was fighting to extricate from Jack's "mind-meld." He was succeeding, starting to sense the moonshiner's angry approach. Jack was feeling negative effects from the medicines; his mind bent with deranged hallucinations, his reflexes slowed, and his coordination off. All that and he had a sick headache with nausea so bad he worried he might throw up. He couldn't remember if they'd gone over what to do if he failed his task. Was there a back-up plan to get 'Moonshine Bob' if this obviously stupid idea of his didn't work?

If he couldn't regain control and the moonshiner wrested the Shoggoth away, …, well, …, that wouldn't be good. His situation would turn from unfortunate to potentially fatal. That much was evident given the size and power of his opponent. He imagined Pop having to explain to his Mom and Dad how he died. And why. The why would be a tough one.

No matter how overmatched he was, Jack knew he couldn't let that happen. He had to survive, if only for his grandfather. He didn't see another way he could help the 'little people' if he scrapped this plan. The best and only thing to do was try his hardest to occupy 'Herman's' head. Of the two demons, the Shoggoth was the most dangerous. It was his idea to do this, and he'd already made a connection, even though it was slipping away.

"Dark thoughts," Jack reminded himself. Summoning them fuels the beast. Malevolent feelings guide it into action. "But that's the problem," he knew. "I don't have them."

"Well, …, better learn," Jack said, resolved to try. He began by thinking how much he hated that his grandfather, without anyone in the family knowing, had kept them safe without any appreciation for his work. He stood alone absorbing ridicule and behind-the-back verbal abuse, friends and family chiding him for his never-ending warnings and curmudgeonly ways. Most of all, he hated how the moonshiner had derailed Pop's possibility of having a normal life.

Jack focused hard on the darkest thoughts he could muster; how mad he was at the unacknowledged sacrifices Pop had made at the cost of his reputation. He allowed himself to come unhinged, a rage hiding deep in his "id." He left his stoicism behind, boiling over in anger.

'Herman' noticed, the creature's head turning, curious. Its gills went wide and it began to circle Jack, wondering where the young man wanted to channel its power. The Shoggoth was once again his to do with as he pleased. It wasn't fighting his effort. But Jack knew it couldn't last. He couldn't "out evil" his counterpart, 'Moonshine Bob'.

Unknown to Jack, his ace-in-the-hole, *Tsul 'Kalu,* was a no show. He couldn't pass the Shoggoth off. But Mr. Joe and the 'little people' knew this could happen - Bigfoot not one to be ordered around - and they planned accordingly. They hadn't told Jack, thinking it might put him under more pressure than he already shouldered.

Speaking of the moonshiner, he'd made it across the cove and saw Jack unguarded. The younger man seemed to have his mind elsewhere, not seeing him approach. 'Herman' was still not responding, and he wondered if it was Jack that was interfering with his connection. He saw his Shoggoth and how it was circling the young man, waiting for orders.

Well, if it was orders the beast wanted, he could easily provide them. This upstart wasn't good at it, 'Moonshine Bob' thought to himself, chuckling. And he knew just what he wanted the beast to do to punish the family.

Joe Cherokee watched from the edge of the deck as 'Moonshine Bob' closed in on the unprepared Jack. Mr. Joe could tell Jack was struggling to hold the monster. Not heeding the pouring rain around him, he removed his poncho, unveiling his traditional Cherokee buckskins and shirt, an homage to his heritage. He raised his eyes to the sky and chanted loudly, honoring his gods.

Looking down, Mr. Joe could tell the moonshiner realized it was Jack in his way. That was good, he thought. It would make the next part of the plan a surprise.

Pop had done his part well. Joe Cherokee was proud of his friend. He'd allowed their opponent to think he'd escaped a trap and now had the advantage. The time had come. Joe Cherokee could reveal his secret part to play in the battle. His last action as a man.

Untying the bandanas around his neck, shedding his shirt, and taking off the leather breeches, Joe unveiled his transformation. Gills on both sides of his neck, fins, and a tail, he was just the thing he'd always tried to become, the embodiment of his brother's designs. And it was time to let 'Moonshine Bob', the anti-Joe Cherokee, the Yang to Joe's Yin, the bad mirroring Joe's good, know he wasn't alone as a freakish, magical mistake. But he had an advantage. He could breathe both in and out of the water.

The Indian leaped into the lake behind 'Moonshine Bob' and applied a chokehold around his neck. The moonshiner reflexively worked to pull Mr. Joe underwater where he knew he'd have an advantage. The depth of the lake plunged acutely down, the two falling together into successively colder layers. But 'Bob's' attacker didn't resist. Down they went, so far down that the water was black with a hint of green, as almost no light filtered through.

'Moonshine Bob' grew more confused the farther they dropped. How could his adversary not let go?

Instead of the deep water drowning the man, the moonshiner himself wasn't breathing well. His neck was in the crotch of his assailant's elbow. More importantly, his gills were mostly blocked as a result. He began to panic. Inexplicably, his attacker let go and spun him around. They were face-to-face, but it was too dark for the weak and choking man-fish to see. Not fighting anymore, the two rose together, nearing the light of the surface.

That's when 'Bob' noticed. His attacker had gills, too. And it wanted him to see.

The two water-breathing men resumed their fight, Joe Cherokee working the moonshiner towards the shore. Joe was the first to touch the sand at the front of the dock, still two body lengths underwater. He dragged his dark reflection to the concrete support posts under the motorized lift for the ski boat. Hanging on to the boat catch above, Joe held 'Bob' in a scissor hold between his stronger thighs, again blocking the gills and strangling him.

Sufficiently weakened, Joe Cherokee let go and pulled the limp 'Bob' up towards the beach. Pop waded in as planned, working his way towards the two men-fish, there to help his friend in their final shared task. Pop pulled 'Moonshine Bob' out by his heels, his head still submerged but quite short of breath from the fight and injuries to his gills. Joe Cherokee secured 'Bob's' arms and joined Pop in dragging the moonshiner to shallow water. Swinging him back and forth by his arms and legs, they gained momentum with each cycle. Finally, they let him go and sent him flying over the rock wall, up on the hillside.

'Moonshine Bob' landed in the underbrush, his mouth making a rhythmic "O" shape as he strained to breathe, out of his element, fish that he was. Trapped in a thicket of rhododendron, he looked over and realized he probably couldn't make it back to the water before he ran out of oxygen.

A fiery wind blew above the moonshiner's head, landing in a shower of sparks behind a large poplar, steps away. Branches of mountain laurel were pushed to the side as if something transparent occupied the space. Out of the void appeared a witch, looking at him hungrily. The scream of a raven came from its mouth. It was *Ka'lanu Ahkyeli'ski*, the *Raven Mocher*, there to collect his heart.

CHAPTER NINETEEN

Jack swam, the metronome of his arms striking the water comfortably fast, with each third stroke a breath. Everything was back to the innocence of earlier that summer, before he knew the secrets of Lake Rabun. His open water training had strengthened his kick, a major goal achieved. Swimming was again Jack's escape, the endorphin rush of vigorous exercise preferable to the adrenaline rush of life-threatening peril.

'Moonshine Bob' had been relegated to the status of make-believe bad guy, now merely a silly meme for visitors to keep safety in mind. Pop was no longer the embarrassing, crotchety, old curmudgeon. He'd been replaced by the kindly and wise "King of the Cove," with "Grams the Queen" no longer having to make excuses for her husband and his "active imagination."

The long training course allowed Jack time, once again, to think. Nowadays, he marveled at the world and its wonders, wondering what else he didn't know that he didn't know. When he wasn't admiring the complexity of God's creation, he was singing again, a break from "thinking too hard." He wasn't Pop, yet. His current song selections had gone more Appalachian, more bluegrass and folk. The rhythm of Alison Krauss's "Down to the River to Pray" matched his current pace perfectly.

" ♫ Come on fathers, let's go down, Let's go down, come on down. Come on fathers let's go down, Down to the river to pray. ♫ " The chorus done, He turned his mind to the future.

College was about to start up again, and he couldn't wait. A female friend on the swim team contacted him the night before. She was a rising sophomore whose mesmerizing butterfly form would, …, uh, …, inspire him. Her long-distance, freshman year boyfriend had, stupidly, Jack thought, left her for another. She called to see if he was unattached, as was the rumor among the girls on the team. Jack wasn't a fan of social media, so she didn't know and couldn't tell from her usual sources.

"Well, it turns out I am," Jack replied, practically jumping into his phone. Pretending to be calm and cool, he kept his voice deep and his conversation relaxed. They arranged to go out after he helped her move into her dorm. She'd never been to Stone Mountain Park, and he liked the trail up the back side of the massive, incongruously situated chunk of granite overlooking downtown Atlanta.

This is more like it, Jack thought. It turns out being a gentleman with respect and boundaries could still work on the opposite sex. Who knew?

Every stroke felt increasingly powerful.

Once again recalling his female friend's perfect butterfly stroke, Jack smiled. His grandparents couldn't complain about her hips. If things worked out, future generations wouldn't get their soft heads squished, traumatized at birth. Swimming while thinking about those hips rising and falling with each lunge in the water, …, it made him less … aerodynamic, …, so to speak. Jack tried to think of something less "inspiring." That, or switch over to backstroke. But then others might notice her effect on him, too.

Necessarily changing subjects, Jack thought again about the end of 'Moonshine Bob' and the part he played. He wondered where his bravery, …, stupidity? …, naivete? came from. He'd been lucky to survive. Wherever it came from, he was proud that his actions helped rid the cove of its curse. Jack had grown up this summer, realizing how trivial his worries were before his awakening.

Jack also made peace with his part in facilitating his friend Joe Cherokee moving on to the "next place." It was necessary and appropriate. It also freed the *Yundwi Tsunsdi* to join their supernatural brothers recharging deep inside the earth.

It was a lot.

Then Jack's thoughts went back to his last memory of Joe Cherokee. With 'Moonshine Bob' dead, Jack freed 'Herman', the Shoggoth shooting away as soon as their connection was lost. It didn't take long for Jack to lose sight of the fish as it disappeared into the depths. Exhausted from his effort to control the beast, he looked over and saw Pop and their Indian friend, still grim-faced from their actions.

Then came a scene Jack played over and over in his mind since it happened. The sight of Mr. Joe leaving this earthly existence. Jack kept his eyes closed under his goggles while he remembered, not caring if he veered off course in his swim.

He relived seeing the Indian's legs, arms, and torso, not to mention his new tail, fins, and gills, dissolve into a fine powder until his face was the last thing left. He was smiling as he melted away, a rainbow of colors spiraling up through the trees. The look on Joe Cherokee's face was so full of love and contentment that it filled Jack's heart despite his sense of loss.

His grandfather called the look "bliss." Mr. Joe's aura reflected joyful acceptance of meeting his fate. It was a look that showed he wanted to see what the Great Spirit had for him next, no matter how mysterious and unknowable.

Jack smiled at the memory. It made him think of a Solzhenitsyn quote Mr. Joe recited the last time they were alone, one of grandfather's favorites. The Russian writer, a prisoner of Stalin's Gulags who was tortured, starved, and denigrated, defied his circumstances. What he put down for history to read was a "Deep Thought" to make other deep thoughts jealous. *"Sometimes I feel quite distinctly that what is inside of me is not all of me. There is something else, sublime, quite indestructible, some fragment of the Universal spirit. Don't you feel that?"*

Joe Cherokee said that this feeling was in him, just as the writer said. He had it with absolute surety. It was undeniable. He could feel it in Jack, as well. And Pop, his friend. He suspected the Universal spirit was in everyone. It made Mr. Joe smile. Jack, too.

Today the feeling Jack had was gratefulness. Swimming in this unique part of God's indescribably beautiful creation, his nearly exhausted miracle-of-a-body performing well through today's training, he knew. There was something inside him, sublime and indestructible, just as the Russian said. Something that intrinsically knew right from wrong, truth from deception, and the value of goodness. Something proven to help arm us to fight evil and assist those in need.

Kicking extra hard the last fifty meters, Jack clanked against the aluminum ladder, the trailing wave he'd created splashed over his shoulders and head. Looking quickly left and right, he'd won again. He climbed the few rungs to the deck and spread out his arms in triumph. Then he fell back again into the cool crisp lake, the water a religious experience indeed.

Pop walked over and looked down at his grandson. He helped him up the ladder, giving a strong grip and a final tug to assist him onto the deck. Jack didn't want to stand, instead sprawling out, the boards still a little too hot from hours of direct sunlight. His chest still heaved catching up on his oxygen deficit, his rate of breathing steadily decreasing as he recovered. Once comfortable, he smiled at his grandfather.

"You would have whipped my butt back in the day," Pop said, returning a look that grandfathers have when they're in awe of their grandsons, not believing something like this could be related to him.

"Still stink at breaststroke," Jack countered, his grin ear-to-ear. "I guess

I inherited that, too."

"Yep. But I stunk at it worse," Pop admitted. "Lots of missed podiums in the IM after I was in the lead after butterfly and backstroke."

Just then, a pair of Jet-Skiers flew by, the curve of their path far too close to the dock. As spray from the crafts shot out towards them and waves shook the dock, they heard the boys Rebel-yell, proud of their devilry.

"God, I hate those things," Jack exclaimed, angry at the two boys and their raucous, callous behavior. "So loud. And those guys take pleasure in terrorizing us. I wish all Jet-Skis were banished from our lake."

Nearly as soon as Jack spoke the words, the boys were thrown ten feet in the air with their Jet-Skis flung against the rocks of the shoreline, breaking into pieces.

After making sure the boys weren't injured, Pop chuckled. "Better be careful what you choose to hate, Jack. Your new friend 'Herman' is listening."